People's reaction to The

"Action packed story in an unusual setting... makes for a good read!"
\qquad M. Lovell

"The plot was very well crafted. Most all of the loose ends were tied up in the end. I liked that!"
\qquad J. Baker

"I particularly appreciated the authentic feeling of the locale and the believability of the action sequences."
\qquad M.G. Stern

Books by Dr. George R. Harker

He Wouldn't Drink the Hemlock: The Firing of Dr. Leisure, 1993

On Second Thought, I'll Drink the Hemlock: The Reinstatement of Dr. Leisure?, 1995

The Intelligent Decision: How We Think!, 1996

Published by **Dr. Leisure**.

The Mammoth Incident

George R. Harker

To Mike & Jennifer
It's a pleasure
with Dr. Leisure

Dr. Leisure
Jan 1998

Dr. Leisure, Macomb, Illinois 61455

To the women and men of the National Park Service who will know the difference between fact and fiction in this book and should find that amusing.

Proceeds from the sale of this book will be used to fight for the concept of academic freedom in institutions of higher learning in Illinois.

Copyright 1995 by George R. Harker

All rights reserved. No part of this book may be reproduced or transmitted in any form or by any means, electronic or mechanical, including photocopying, recording, or by any information storage and retrieval system, without permission in writing from the publisher.

Published by:

Dr. Leisure
13 Cedar Drive
Macomb, Illinois 61455-1247

309-837-4160

Manufactured in the United States of America

ISBN 0-9638802-7-6   Paperbound

Library of Congress Catalog Card Number: 95-92087

10 9 8 7 6 5 4 3 2 1

First 1995 Edition

Chapter One

The blows were quick and unexpected, each blow hitting with a precision only a few highly disciplined martial arts enthusiasts can ever hope to achieve.

It seemed like a slow motion ballet as the two lifeless forms crumpled and pitched over the edge of the rock outcropping from which only moments before they had both enjoyed the view; one of those pleasant and bucolic views known to almost anyone who has hiked the low mountains and hills of southern Kentucky around Mammoth Cave.

Ken and Lissy were out enjoying the back packing they had both grown to love when undergraduates at Southern Kentucky State. Since they had entered grad school and started living together, they really looked forward to these chances to "get away" and experience nature. Death was the farthest thought from their minds when they eased up to the edge of the outcropping for a better view of the valley below. All in all, the spot looked quite nice for their trail lunch of wine, fruit, cheese and crackers.

They had not seen and would now not ever see the figures below, moving materials from a cream colored Dodge van into an opening in the hillside. The opening was adjacent to a large massive wood door enforced with steel bands and bolts. The door was one of a few in the park that secured entrances to Mammoth Cave which the National Park Service did not want used by the general public but occasionally might need to be entered by Park Service personnel.

George R. Harker

The lock on the chain which had secured the hefty door lay opened in the dirt. It had not been forced but had given up its hold on the two steel links because someone had a key or because of a little coaxing from a skilled hand. Actually the latter was the case since the people moving in and out of the cave were not National Park Service personnel.

"Hurry, bring the explosives. Be more careful. Dropping isn't supposed to affect this stuff but no need to find out to the contrary first hand, " a man directed with that air of self that would suggest the leader at any function.

"If you don't like the way I am doing it, you can always do it yourself, " said the woman inside the van as she slid a crate toward the door opening. The respondent was strikingly different from the others, a woman of about thirty with a trim figure and long brown hair. Her outfit of designer jeans and sweater top would have won acceptance at any cocktail party as well as in this wooded hollow. A third member of the group returning from the cave to get another load had a Neanderthal quality sharply contrasting the beauty of the woman.

This individual was obviously not one of those in possession of a superior intellect. But what ever was lacking in intelligence was obviously offset by bulk, not bulk of unrestrained fat cells but rather masses of muscle tissue holding a massive frame together.

The impact of the bodies on the hillside above

The Mammoth Incident

had dislodged a small boulder which in turn had dislodged a couple of other rocks of lesser size which tumbled down the hillside. One of these ended its travel in front of the van. The Neanderthal man detoured from his original path and picked up the fifty pound rock and threw it off to one side with ease.

"Did he have to do that?" asked the lady.

"Do what?" questioned the leader intent on the job immediately at hand and apparently unaware of the actions which had just occurred on the hillside above.

"Kill those people!" retorted the lady.

"Oh, pity. He has his orders. It was problematical. As you are aware, we can not risk being identified and associated with this entrance to the cave. We took a calculated risk that no one would see us here today. It is not his fault those two came along when they did. Another few minutes and we would have been gone," said the leader. "Come on and give me a hand. All the more reason we need to get out of here as fast as we can."

Another two crates were hurriedly moved into the cave. The heavy door was swung closed and the chain and lock restored. The large man found a small bush and uprooted it. Then proceeded to brush over the tracks made by the group as they moved in and out of the cave. When finished he joined the others in the van.

"Let's get out of here and pick up our karate expert before someone else shows up. The Park

George R. Harker

Service will be hard pressed to explain the accidental death of two hikers. The addition of any more may be more coincidental than even they can explain," said the leader as he shifted into first gear and the van lurched down the narrow access road.

Chapter Two

Washington D. C.

The office of the special services branch of the National Park Service is tucked away in a corner of the CIA complex west of Washington. To those with no particular business with this branch of the Service it is generally unknown. While the name appears on the basic flow chart of the Park Service the money allocated to it seems rather minuscule compared to the other activities of the Service. But financial statements and public budgets can be deceptive when funds for the operational aspect of the office draw from the same coffers as the CIA.

The office was strictly upper echelon government, with lots of windows, and a large bureaucratic desk with the seal of the United States on the front. An American flag stood in one corner of the room and the Park Service insignia in the other. In other words one of those sterile bureaucratic offices with every thing in its place and to all appearances a place where nothing was or ever would be accomplished.

Camden entered, he had been picked up at the airport by the "store" limousine. Treatment he knew meant the meeting was more than an afternoon tea. Usually he had to flip for the cab fare and stand in line to get one at that. Something was in the wind to bring him back from his Jamaican holiday only a week in progress.

"Come in Camden, we've been expecting you,"

remarked Jim Baker, acting chief of Special Services.

"Camden this is Pete Conrad, head narc in the Appalachian region."

"Pete meet Mick Camden, Special Services operative."

"A pleasure, I've heard a lot about you in the last few days. Your reputation has preceded you."

"Don't believe every thing you hear. Tell me what's with the drug business and bringing me back from that cute redhead in Jamaica. I was just getting to know my way around . . . the island of course."

"Didn't you read that briefing file I sent down?" inquired the chief.

"Of course, but I hardly see how the accidental death of two young graduate students becomes a service matter."

"The deaths were listed as accidental on the death certificate and that is the information that was given out to the press. Interestingly, the public seemed to buy the story. If they didn't like the press version they seemed contented with the rumor we planted that it was a lover suicide pact." Jim continued, " The ranger that found the bodies has been with us long enough to believe this area is relatively free from this sort of fall. The overlook is situated such that it takes some effort to accidentally fall and the likelihood of both falling seemed improbable. The autopsy indicated both had broken necks. A mark on approximately the same place on each suggest the blows were administered by some agent other than the

The Mammoth Incident

rocks below."

"We feel that the killings were drug related. Recently there has been a lot of drug activity in the area. The locals have developed a strain of marijuana that surpasses 'Acapulco Gold' in quality. The demand has been so strong that virtually every square inch of cultivatable land has been put to use. Each planting may be very small, but when enough are tucked into the numerous nooks and crannies of every mountainside, it starts to add up."

"We're not sure what the details are. Perhaps these kids came across a group loading up a recent crop and people got nervous. Some high placed people in the local community are known to be involved, but would like to believe it is not known and will do any thing to keep it that way. On the other hand perhaps these individuals were involved directly as suppliers or buyers who could not meet expenses. There are other possibilities. The main thing is that this killing is not the first in a series of unsolved murders on government property in this region. Its becoming a political problem as well as an embarrassment to the Park Service. People getting wiped out by grizzly's every once in a while adds to the mystic aspect of wilderness. Humans killings human isn't quite as acceptable," Baker explained.

"Your job is to locate and break-up the organization behind this drug ring. Any questions?"

"When do I start?" inquired Camden.

"Good, the response we were anticipating,"

replied Pete.

"The limo that brought you here is out front and ready to take you to the airport. A Park Service uniform and other gear is on the plane waiting. Good luck," noted Pete.

"A chartered plane, isn't that a bit excessive for the Park Service?" asked Camden.

"It does sound a bit melodramatic, actually we have a shipment of needed radio parts that have to be sent there quickly and a charter was as cheap as airfreight. It just happens to correspond with your transportation needs." Jim Baker's smile indicated the plane was more closely tied to the organization than his remarks suggested. Camden didn't need to know that, so would not be told, at least not directly.

"I though the James Bond aura was a bit much. I'll be on my way."

"One more thing for what its worth. There is a rumor of sorts that a group of 'university types' is into the world terrorist movement. Probably just a lunatic pseudo intellectual group looking for something to do on weekends and of no significance to this situation."

The black limo would have been conspicuous in Midwest America, but racing down the freeway toward Washington airport it was just one of many, basically indiscernible from the others. Except for the alpha numeric configuration of the license plate. The plate was not an imaginative combinations of letters and numbers such as often adorn limos parked on the

The Mammoth Incident

"hill." A rather modest nondescript "QR-4" adorned this buggy. The edges of the plate were beginning to rust for that matter. So much for class.

The airport exit sign appeared momentarily, loomed large, and then disappeared as the car kept pace with traffic and merged right to exit.

The driver slowed in consideration of the posted ramp speed and the overly sharp break to the right that mandated such a maneuver if one did not want to pick guard rails out of the radiator.

The driver cursed softly as he applied further braking to avoid the Mercedes pulled off on the edge of the road but still with a portion of the car overhanging the pavement. A jack under the rear bumper suggested the motorist's plight.

Mick thought the sound of pavement rumble strips a bit loud for such a large and soundproof car.

The first bullet caught Mick's driver in the throat. The rest that followed worked a pattern across the windshield. The cluster reaching the back seat compartment left little room for movement or any basis to doubt their intent.

The car straightened from the previously directed course and sped straight forward. Missing the parked Mercedes by inches, but not the break-away-light pole. The space trip was brief as the four ton vehicle nosed into the water trap at the number four hole of Edgewater Country Estates.

Why the car would burn with the engine and potential source of ignition buried in the primeval mud would be hard for the professional engineers to explain. Nevertheless, a fire ball and muted explosion engulfed the portion of the vehicle above the waterline.

Edgewater Estates would be needing new resident swans.

Chapter Three

The takeoff, delayed a couple of hours was uneventful. The twin turboprops whined reassuringly as the plane gained momentum and rolled down the runway with ever increasing speed. Camden sat back and tried to relax, noting a number of sore muscles of which he had previously not been aware.

The rescue crew had dragged him from the back seat of the limousine thinking he was surely dead from the explosion. Being dead, gentleness gave way to ease and efficiency in pulling the "body" through the blown out rear window. However, he wasn't dead. In fact he had only passed out from the concussion of hitting the back of the front seat as the blast hurled inward. The main force had deflected upward and away from the passenger compartment.

The whole thing was a bit of an embarrassment for Jim Baker. The limousine was being road tested by the garage to determine if the power steering was now working properly. The car was used exclusively by the second in command of the CIA, usually. Needing the road test, Jason at the garage had sent the limousine down when Baker had requested a car to the airport.

Once the determination had been made that Camden was in one piece, the only obvious decision was to continue as if nothing had happened. The FBI would have to deal with their own problem with regard to the occupants of the Mercedes.

The engine whine diminished slightly as the plane reached altitude and leveled off. Camden, grabbed a beer from the built in refrigerator and settled back for the one hour flight. The lights of Washington fading over the horizon as the plane headed southwest.

It hadn't seemed like an hour, but then Camden hadn't been awake the whole time either. A voice over the intercom brought Camden to his senses and he moved forward into the cockpit.

"Coast Guard reports a DC-3 moving in from the Atlantic at a low altitude and not in radio contact with flight control," said soft spoken Jim King. Jim had the slow drawl of a west Texan and the lanky frame to match. A Vietnam veteran that flew B 52's in Nam, he flew for the special services now in the guise of a private charter line. A bit tame since heat seeking missiles weren't yet in vogue in the states like they had been in Nam. "Customs knows we're here and asked us to shadow the guy if its not a problem. What's your pleasure?"

"Why not?" Camden replied, "nothing else to do up here and I am already four hours late as it is."

"Thought you might say that. That's an affirmative, Whiskey Zulu in pursuit of suspect. Switching to frequency 128.5 for further instructions," King acknowledged to the ground station.

The initial visual contact with the suspect aircraft was innocuous enough. A giant gray shadowed silhouette moving over the ground just above treetop level far below the left wing tip. Although the silhouette was softened by the distance it was to the

The Mammoth Incident

trained observer unmistakable as a DC-3, that vintage work horse of aviation well known for its cargo carrying ability in World War II.

Camden didn't know the difference, but then he wasn't the resident expert either.

"It's a DC-3. Looks like the `ghost ship' they flew in Nam," remarked King. "They used to load those babies up with electric drive Gatling guns that could put a thousand rounds through a target in the time it takes to sneeze."

"Is that my imagination, or did he just turn on some lights. I don't understand," said Camden.

"Apparently, he figures he has cleared the coast and that it will attract less suspicion if he acts like a regular aircraft. Anyone else flying tonight will have the running lights on. The timing is fortunate. It will make our job a lot easier." King acknowledged as he throttled back the twin turboprops in an effort to not out fly the leisurely moving DC-3 below.

"Target flying a heading of two-six-zero. Approximate airspeed 150 mile per hour. Just over Shenandoah National Park. Request further instructions," radioed King.

"Hold your position such that you can follow to home, if possible. Watch for chutes or any other sign of a drop," replied ground control. "We don't want to lose this one, if we can help it."

King radioed a willingness to pursue the target aircraft and continued to monitor its lumbering flight over the Appalachians for the next forty-five minutes.

George R. Harker

No chutes where observed and the direction of flight did not change. And the excitement of being involved in shadowing a possible drug smuggler seemed far removed from the actual realities of doing it, Camden reflected to himself. The forty-five minutes of nothingness was beginning to bother King as well. The turbo-prop was not running at its designed airspeed or peak efficiency. While not particularly detrimental to the aircraft, it did bother King who was a perfectionist when it came to flying.

King radioed ground control, "This target could fly all night, do you have any idea where the drop zone may be?"

"Negative, have no idea where drop zone is. If you have to get going we understand and appreciate your help to this point," ground control responded.

"How about we get the numbers off that aircraft? Would that help?" asked King.

"Affirmative, but surely you jest?" Came a rather sardonic and questioning ground control.

"Not really, we'll make a short jaunt to the North and then swing down South at his approximate altitude. We can pass close enough to catch the numbers and he will think we are just another bird in the air taking a girl friend for a moonlight ride," King explained.

"You got it. Gook Luck," ground control acknowledged.

As the throttles moved toward the fire wall the whine of the turboprops increased in pitch and the

The Mammoth Incident

airspeed picked up dramatically. Based on some seat of the pants dead reckoning King put the plane North far enough that it would not be visible to the DC-3 if it had been observed at all. A new course was set in a direction designed to intersect in approximately five minutes. Camden sat quietly watching King deafly put the aircraft through maneuvers. Camden was not a pilot and really had no interest in the multitude of gauges, levers, and switches that King obviously knew intimately.

"Get the night scope from that compartment behind the seat. I just happen to have one with me. You never know when it will come in handy," mused King. " Another minute or so and we'll be close enough. . . There, just to your left and slightly above us."

Just as Camden bought the scope onto target, an orange flash and a cloud of smoke filled the field of view. In the same instant Camden felt the aircraft roll and dive with an abruptness the senses could not fully register. Somewhere during the slow motion account of these events in the mind a shouted "hang on" was recorded from King.

The slow motion imagery continued. Including the view of treetops looming ever larger as the aircraft headed for the ridge line which only moments before had been hundreds of feet below, but now could be measured with a folding ruler. Above and behind Camden's right ear the sound of a muffled explosion could be heard over the wine of the engines. The imagery also included King, just barely perceptible off in the corner of Camden's field of vision. The ever increasing size of the indigenous pine had his undivided attention at the moment.

The right wing-tip slapped the topmost five inches of one tree and then a little less of another. In another instant Camden began to sense that the trees were no longer vertical to the ground but were now at right angles to his perception of perpendicular. Sensed because before Camden's consciousness could register, the spatial relationships had changed again.

Up ahead the hard darkness of clear sky appeared where moments before the soft muffled darkness of pine covered ridges had been. Years of experience in Vietnam had developed the skills in King that few pilots even know could exist let alone hope to achieve. The heat seeking missile had missed literally by inches.

King pulled back at the precise rate needed to clear the next ridge by little more than inches and continued to climb to an altitude more respectable for a turboprop of this configuration. The controls seemed working the way they were intended and the engines were functioning flawlessly. King was thankful for this but couldn't help wondering how many shrapnel holes were scattered about the fuselage and wing surfaces. After all repairs of this sort cost money and while insurance may cover hail damage it wold be hard to convince an adjuster hail could be this sharp. But then why worry, King's "insurance adjuster"

The Mammoth Incident

worked for a company subsidized by the same outfit that kept King in the air.

As the plane gained altitude and the surrounding topography took on the perspectives usually associate with 5,000 feet of altitude, the radio began to function.

"Station 5 calling Whiskey two three Zulu. Station 5 calling Whiskey two three Zulu. Do you copy?" came the professional unruffled tone of the ground controller.

"Station 5 this Whiskey two three Zulu. Go ahead," a smiling King responded.

"What happened? We were afraid you had gone down."

"Almost, just a little CAT action. Will fill you in on the land line. Target has been lost. Proceeding to destination as originally planned, unless other instructions. Whiskey two three Zulu." King replied wondering how the clear air turbulence explanation would be received by the ground station or others which might be monitoring the frequency.

The remaining fifteen minutes of flight time were uneventful. The small field that served Mammoth Cave National Park or more specifically the community of Possum Run was not exceptional but adequate as fields go and presented no difficulties to the average pilot let along one of King's skill. In fact the strong cross wind added an element to the approach that raised the event an incremental amount above mundane.

On the ground, a pale green National Park Service pickup truck pulled adjacent to the aircraft.

As Camden stepped down the ladder he was greeted by a slightly rotund man. "You must be Camden. I'm Bill Hicks, park superintendent. How was your flight?"

"Not bad, except for the CAT. . . Clear air turbulence, atmospheric conditions that you can't see on radar but which can toss a plane around like a cork. Never knew of them until tonight. Just about put us in the mountain," Camden explained knowingly for a person just acquainted with the concept and never with the actual phenomenon itself.

King avoided looking at Camden directly not wanting to strain the credibility of the cover-up with an untimely smile.

"Where do you want these supplies?" inquired King of superintendent Hicks.

"Leave them till morning. I'll send a crew out... You must be Jim King, pilot extraordinary. Headquarters said you would be at the controls," noted Hicks.

"Forgive me, this is indeed Jim King. And I readily support that idea of 'pilot extraordinary.' He put that plane through some maneuvers you wouldn't believe," reiterated Camden with an air of conviction that wasn't forced in any way.

"I understand you don't like to let that baby sit out," Hicks commented while gesturing toward the turboprop, "even overnight. With that thought in mind

The Mammoth Incident

I made arrangements for you to have hanger 2 for tonight. Its the one on the other end of the apron next to that DC-3."

Both men glanced at the DC-3, then at each other and then back to the plane. It couldn't be. Just a coincidence, as popular as DC-3 once were there are an awful lot of them about. However, when time permitted it was something to check out just in case.

A few more minutes and the turboprop was secured in hanger 2 and the three men headed down the twisting mountain road which lead from the relatively flat plateau on which the airport was perched.

"This drug business is getting out of hand. It was one thing when a few locals cultivated a few patches of marijuana in some rarely travelled back corner of the park. The unofficial attitude was to look the other way if on a patrol a ranger ran across a patch. Often the patches were so small you couldn't always be sure it didn't get established on its own. The stuff has grown wild around here for years." Hicks sighed, "But things changed a while back. The so called patches started getting bigger and more numerous. The strain being cultivate was more potent, requiring more attention as well as demanding more money in the marketplace. The people growing it were not doing it for themselves. Dollars were involved, and big dollars at that."

Hicks continued as the Dodge leisurely rolled down the hillside, almost driving itself. Much as an old horse heads back to the barn after a long day in the field. "A week ago one of the rangers brought in a bunch of poppies. They weren't a local variety. These were premium grade opium types. . . "

The roar of an automobile making time could be heard down the valley mixed with the shrill of a police siren. In the time it took the Dodge to ease onto the road shoulder a pair of headlights came into view and loomed ever closer at a high rate of speed. In another instant the `51 Hudson Hornet shot past doing something in excess of seventy-five. An incredible speed given the winding road and the lose surface. Not thirty seconds behind came a late model four door sedan with a rack of flashing red and white lights. Not to mention the air piercing siren whining at full till. Emblazoned on the side in reflective letters illuminated by the glare of the Dodge's lights were the letters "s", "h", "e", "r", "i", "f", "f".

Within seconds the two cars passed from sight as they snaked around the bend and up the valley. The siren fading as rapidly as it had increased in volume on the approach. The three men sat quietly. Two in questioning disbelief, wondering what they had just witnessed.

Although it had only been a minute, it did seem the action was over and time to move on, prompting King to suggest as much.

"Just a second, its not over yet," Hicks replied with an air of confidence that conveyed a knowledge of events not known to the other two men.

The Mammoth Incident

Although it seemed longer it actually was only five minutes and the roar of a motor could be heard from up the valley. In less time then it takes to tell headlights knifed through the trees as a vehicle hurdled down the valley. In another moment the `51 Hudson rocketed past the Dodge pelting it with a shower of gravel and dirt as if to show its contempt.

Still Hicks made no attempt to proceed down the valley. This time King knew better than to ask. He merely resigned himself to wait and see what was going to happen next. While the wait seemed longer than the actual five minutes, it wasn't. The light of a single beam cut through the trees as the second car returned down the valley. This time the sheriff's car was traveling at a much more guarded speed. The right headlight fractured badly by whatever made the vertical crease which ran from bumper to hood. While it may have been an illusion it did seem to Camden that the flashing lights on the rack were not rotating as fast as before. The siren was mute, of that there could be no dispute.

As the taillights of the sheriff's car passed from view, Hicks put the Dodge back on the road and headed down the valley as if nothing had really happened at all.

Camden broke the silence, "Well, what's the story? It's not everyday you see a `51 Hudson outrunning the police."

"Isn't that the truth," added King obviously sharing Camden's disbelief over the events of the last few minutes.

"Historically it goes back to the days when moonshine was the big illegal money maker in this area. The locals would make it in the hills where they knew the law would never find them. To get it to market they started using hopped up cars with concealed tanks containing the moonshine. That assumes they weren't running on it... The market for the homegrown stuff fell out years ago as grain prices went out of sight and the need for the special talents of mechanics and drivers also diminished. However, the thrill of the chase seemed to really get into the blood of some of these folks that they have developed it, the fast car and the chase, into a rather sophisticated leisure activity. There is a secret club which puts a semi-vintage car on the highway at least once a month looking for a confrontation with the sheriff or any other law enforcement type willing to take them on. You just had the rare opportunity to view the encounter first hand," smiled Hicks.

"It sounds like they don't lack for excitement around here," reflected Camden. "I though hill folk lived a rather tranquil life watching the world go by from the rocking chair on the front porch."

"These roads aren't safe to drive with crackpots like that rolling around. I'll stick to flying. It's safer," exclaimed King looking for a rise from Camden that he knew would not be forthcoming.

Chapter Four

It was not the typical plantation house usually associated with the deep south, but instead a structure with all the trappings of an English manor house. Not really surprising given that it was built after the civil war by a retired British sea captain that had decided to retire away from the influence of the Crown. At least away from the tax influence of the Crown. All other aspects of "civilized" British living of the time were incorporated into the style and operation of the manor house and the adjacent 14 acres of formal gardens.

Hicks supplied other bits of background information on the manor house and its occupants as he drove Mick to the reception and open house. The major held these events periodically and it was almost compulsory that the resident park superintendent attend. Actually Hicks didn't mind at all. His slightly rotund figure gave some indication of how he and food got along. The spread this evening would be far more exotic than the usual fare he managed to pick up at the food concessions in the park or the local dinners.

"Major I would like you to meet Mick Camden. Mick has just joined our staff in a ranger capacity," said Hicks shaking hands with a very trim and athletic man of about fifty. A man with a six foot stature who exuded an air of command which seemed very much in keeping with being addressed as Major. "Mick this Major Kenneth Henderson, retired Army. As you might have guessed, everybody calls him

George R. Harker

Major."

"Pleased to meet you sir. The superintendent has told me of your contributions and efforts in support of the park. It is an honor to make your acquaintance," said Camden thinking about some of the other things that Hicks had told him and his briefing in Washington a few days before. Only time would tell if there was more to the Major than met the eye. In any event he certainly came across as an individual that could take charge if necessary.

"Don't believe everything Bill tells you about me. I am sure that whatever I have done for the park would be done by most anyone else if they had my means. Besides as they say you can't take it with you," said the Major. "I am always happy to meet the new park rangers. I am somewhat envious of you people. In my day ranger didn't have quite the same connotation. I would have much preferred working in a National Park over some of the places I've been... . Thinking you might be interested in seeing more of the grounds than most of my guests, I have arranged for one of my daughters, Sarah, to show you around. I hope I have not been too presumptuous."

"No, not at all. I would very much like to see the grounds. I am most impressed with what little I have seen so far just on the drive in, " said Camden. "Where can I find your daughter?"

"She will find you as soon as she is available. I told her you would be with Bill so she knows how to find you," replied the Major in a matter consistent

The Mammoth Incident

with the idea that he indeed was in charge and had everything in control down to the last detail.

"Father insisted I show you around the grounds," a smiling dark haired beauty remarked to Camden as he stepped past the reception line and entered the main foyer. "I was reluctant having given this tour so many times I am beginning to feel like a tour guide. However, you are not the elderly gentleman that my father led me to expect. Presumably one of his little jokes."

"You must be Sarah. I, too, am pleasantly surprised. The superintendent mentioned the Major had daughters but did not go into details. . . I was expecting someone in pigtails."

"This way, let me show you around the gardens and introduce you to some of the other guests," she moved through the French doors onto an extensive patio of cut stone. A number of tables were set out with a variety of hors d'oeuvres and wine. A number of assorted servants moved from table to table restocking whatever delicacy was becoming in short supply.

"Madame Clarette, may I introduce Mick Camden. Mick this is Madame Clarette. Mick is with the National Park Service at Mammoth Cave. He has just arrived this week, as a matter of fact," explained Sarah. "Madame Clarette is the Mayor of Littleburg. Just a few miles down the road."

A few pleasantries with the Mayor and a few more introductions later Camden found himself escorted toward the perimeter of the formal garden.

"Not everything here dates to the 1870's. Father had some `civilized conveniences' of his own added," intimated Sarah. "This is by far my favorite. A place where I can get away with my own thoughts and truly relax. . . . It's not on the stock house and grounds tour, but I sense you may like it."

The stone path through the garden forked and cut back on itself into a rather dense stand of laurel bushes. A weathered gate of cedar and wrought iron moved easily on its hinges as Sarah pushed the latch and applied pressure. Within the enclosure defined by the laurel bushes and other plants was a round pool of approximately eight feet in diameter. Wisps of water vapor rose from the surface suggesting a water temperature higher than the usual swimming pool. Sarah hit an insulated switch adjacent to the gate and the hydro jets surged the water from a tranquil calmness to an inviting broth of air and water.

"Father's hot tub. I don't know when he last used it, but I get out here when ever I can," said Sarah.

"Very nice. I agree one of the more `civilized' amenities of current times," Camden concurred.

"Come on, we have time for a dip. Father is too busy entertaining to miss us and we won't be disturbed," whispered Sarah as she slipped the bolt on the gate and moved toward the pool.

Before Camden could respond, Sarah had slipped out of her garments which she discarded in a

The Mammoth Incident

heap on the deck chair near the gate. Camden could do no more than glimpse the fine contours of her well formed body as she stepped gracefully into the caldron of bubbling water. Her taut breasts slipping below the surface as she sat down.

Camden slipped as quickly from his clothes as he could while trying to capture the full rapture of the sight he thought he had just seen. While no stranger to beautiful women, the ambience and the shared energy could not be ignored. As he slipped into the pool he knew the temperature of the water would be rising from the suggested normal hot tub temperature of 102 degrees Fahrenheit.

Few words were spoken as the sun dipped behind the pines to the west. Bits and pieces of party sounds drifted into the area occasionally barely audible above the action of the water.

The brush of semi floating arms gave way to a lingering embrace. Sarah's body seemed to float from a position adjacent to Camden's to directly in front. As she settled onto his lap she gently guided his rigid protrusion between her receptive thighs. Camden's mind began to keep harmony with the lapping of the waters until it surged to become one with the universe as a simultaneous convulsion of pleasure shook Sarah.

The therapeutic value of hot tubing was not lost on Camden. However, all good things must come to an end and the superintendent would be wondering what happened to Camden. After all, Camden was here to get acquainted with the Major and other influential people in the community. Anybody that was anybody would be at the Major's reception.

Relaxed in a manner that words could not adequately describe the two returned to the manor house to "circulate" and "get acquainted."

Chapter Five

The explosion occurred twenty minutes after the three o'clock tour of the main section of Mammoth cave had begun. The tour was lead by rangers Smith and Jones. Leading the group through one of the more traveled sectors of the cave the chain of events about to unfold were not anticipated and indeed could not have been anticipated by even the most skilled park guide.

The explosion was rather muffled as explosions go. It would be obvious later that the placement of the charges had been done by an expert. Maximum results would be achieved by the minimum amount of charge.

A section of the ceiling collapsed in the larger room just up and around the bend. Tons of limestone which had stood silent and unmovable for millions of years now moved under an ominous force. The passage ahead was choked by large and small boulders that would take days to remove.

The shock wave, as might be expected, caught the rangers and indeed everyone in the group by surprise. Within seconds of the shock wave came a mixture of air and dust forced through the passage by the force of the blast. The group of thirty tourist and two rangers found themselves lying on the floor in a tangled mass of intertwined arms and legs. It would take a few minutes to determine that with one exception physical injuries were minimal. Right at the moment everyone was too stunned to know just what their situation was much less the person's next to them.

While it seemed longer, it was only within three minutes that another explosion occurred. This time the explosion was behind the group and occurred in the passage they had left only minutes before. The shock wave and the blast of dust was not as forceful. Dissipated in part by the bend in the passage and also perhaps because a smaller charge had been used. But who among those trapped could be conscious of such subtle differences? Sheer terror gripped all with a grasp that threatened life itself.

On the surface a slight tremor passed quickly through the cabin where Camden reviewed a recent report from Washington. Only Camden's subconscious picked up the barely perceptible shaking of the ground on which the cabin was situated. Within minutes Camden's consciousness was brought to bear on the frantic movement outside his cabin. These were the sounds of frenzied voices and scurrying feet all moving toward the historic entrance of the cave.

One set of footsteps stopped at Camden's door. A knock intended as an introduction and not as a request to answer the door proceeded ranger Tim Clark.

"Come quick, there has been an accident at the cave. A cave-in... People are trapped, maybe killed," gasped Clark between quick breaths.

Camden nodded and followed Clark to the cave entrance. A small group was gathering around the Superintendent who was assigning tasks to

The Mammoth Incident

different men. "Joe you and Ed take five men and get down there with shovels and picks. Get digging if possible but be careful about the danger of rock slides. Send Bill back with your assessment of the situation. I will be in the office coordinating things from this end."

Camden caught the Superintendent's eye, "How about I go with them chief?"

"All right, I am sure they can use another hand on those shovels," responded the Superintendent. "Just watch for falling rocks."

The team moved out grabbing lanterns, shovels and picks which had just been brought up in a pickup from the maintenance shed. Heading down the steps of the historic entrance they were gratified to find that the power was still on and the light system was working. The light quality left something to be desired however, as the air was filled with a fine dust that created diffuse halos around each fixture. The dust didn't help breathing either, but was tolerable to men with a purpose.

Down the passage and around the bend the group moved at a very swift walk just short of a run. Joe and Ed taking the lead had just rounded the last turn obscuring the fall.

"Look at that, a couple hundred tons of ceiling must have given way. If people were under that when it went down they wouldn't stand a chance," exclaimed Joe.

"You're right enough but we have to try.

Sometimes air pockets are formed and through sheer luck people survive, if dug out before suffocating," countered Ed. "You two, start over here, be careful, there may be people in here. Move as much as you can as fast as you can but keep a look out for arms, legs what have you."

Within seconds the full compliment of men was deployed and digging with a controlled frenzy. They were intent on only one thing, finding survivors. That is of course if there were survivors.

"Stop digging!"

The crews stopped for an instant and then resumed. Surely they had not heard the command to stop digging.

"Stop digging," this time there could be no doubt. Their ears had not deceived them. The sound filled the cave. It was louder than any of them were capable of speaking without some amplification equipment. Indeed the voice seemed to be coming from one or more speakers within the cave.

"What the Hell," exclaimed Joe as all froze in position not believing but not proceeding without clarification.

"Put down your shovels. There is nothing you can do here. Leave as you have come and no harm will come to you." Intoned the monotone blaring out of the concealed speakers.

"Keep digging, " Joe yelled to the men.

The statues came back to life and started where they had left off moments before.

The Mammoth Incident

"I will not tell you again... Stop digging and leave the cave... There is nothing you can do here. To stay is to die," came the ominous voice on the loud speakers.

A small explosion just up the passage from where the men were standing dislodged a boulder from a shelf of the cave. A shelf where the boulder had probably not moved for thousands of years. The boulder wobbled and rolled down the side of the cave until coming to rest against an iron pipe fence which bordered the walkway.

To suggest that the boulder's movement had the attention of the group would be an understatement. All eyes were riveted to the spot. If mental energy was all that was needed to levitate matter there surely was enough present to move a boulder ten times larger.

Camden too had his attention focused on the boulder. Unlike the others he didn't dwell on the movement of the rock once it was clear that the course of travel would end in the iron pipe. He quickly scanned the area around the base of where the boulder had sat and noted a fine black line heading down the cave wall in the direction of the walkway.

"That is just a sample. Leave the cave now or die," the voice commanded.

Joe motioned to the men to follow. All did save Camden who eased into the shadows near the boulder which had just been dislodged.

Camden could hear the sound of the men

diminishing rapidly as they left the passage and headed toward the historic entrance and the way out. He wished he was with them. But first things first and his immediate attention was drawn to the "black line", the wire he had observed moments before.

Camden moved cautiously and quietly from his hiding point in the shadows when he could no longer hear the men moving over the pounding of his own heart. The wire was only discernable for about three feet and then disappeared in the sand and other debris of the cave floor. The exposed portion apparently was revealed by the force of the explosion.

Bending over to more closely examine the exposed portion of the wire, Camden heard a soft whirring sound over his left shoulder. In less time than it took to turn toward the sound, a second explosion rocked the silence. A boulder on the opposite side of the cave dislodged and rolled.

"Leave or die!" boomed the loudspeakers.

Camden knew when to take the hint and moved rapidly to join the rest who were well on their way out of the cave. He did manage to pick up a souvenir on the way, about a foot of black wire.

Chapter Six

Camden and Jim McCoy sat in Superintendent Hicks' office. A rather unimposing place tucked off a corridor on the second floor of the main visitor center. A flag stood in one corner of the room and a collection of photographs of wild flowers ornamented the wall. The shelves contained a number of bound plans for the park. Some dated to 1920 just a few years after the cave had been acquired by the government.

"It was in the morning mail. It actually arrived about the time of the blast and of course in all the confusion it was overlooked until a few minutes ago when my secretary decided cave-in or not, someone had to tend to the shop," Hicks spoke in his normal low keyed tone of voice.

"So it is 10 million transferred to an offshore bank or the roof drops in on 40 . . . Do we know how many are down there yet?" McCoy noted passing a single sheet of paper held between two layers of Mylar, taped at the edges.

Camden glanced at the ransom note and laid it on the table.

"We can't say for certain just how many people are down there. All we really know is that rangers Smith and Jones are there. They were on duty and scheduled to lead the tour. This time of day usually involves between 30 and 60 visitors depending on the choice of trail they want to walk. This particular tour is considered one of the easiest to make and quite popular with all ages. I don't see how we can know just how many or who is down there unless we can make contact with the group."

"Can that be done?" asked Camden.

"Theoretically," noted Hicks. "We have phone lines running throughout the main portion of the cave used by the public. Some of the lines were damaged by the blast or otherwise tampered with but we are still checking and may be able to find one intact. . . then again we may not. . ."

"Have you notified Washington?" asked Camden knowing the answer but wanting to make some conversation while his mind raced to sort out the strange series of events that were unfolding about him.

"Is there any other way in or out of that portion of the cave?" asked Camden.

Hicks turned to a detailed engineering drawing of the cave pulled from one of the master plans of an earlier decade. This had been taped to a portion of the wall after removing some eight by ten color prints of Alaskan wild flowers. "For all intents and purposes, no. The main exit and entrance was the one followed by the established rout. Incidentally, this section of the cave is probably one of the first portions opened to the public and consequently probably the most visited of the entire system."

"You said for all intents and purposes. What did you mean by that?" inquired Camden. His curiosity raised by Hicks' choice of words.

"Well, as in many other parts of the cave there

The Mammoth Incident

are passages entering along the main corridor. Some of these are quite small but there are others that a man might squeeze through... At least this is the usual situation in many parts of the cave. In point of fact I do not know for sure whether this portion of the cave has such passages or not... You see this portion of the cave is generally taken for granted. It has been known so long and traveled through by so many off to search the unexplored portions of the cave that it has been virtually overlooked for fifty years," Hicks explained.

"Is there any way we can get a handle on these passages?" asked Camden.

"It may be a long shot but if there is a record it should be contained within the documentation in this room. Most serious cave explorers were pretty good about keeping records on what they were exploring. Let's put Mitchel on it. He has more of an interest in the historical aspects of this cave than some of our other people and poked around a lot in the archives working on some new interpretative exhibits for the visitor center. He is also one competent spelunker," Hicks noted. "That would be a sweet trick if we can pull it off. Find some other passage and waltz everybody through it while we stall the extortionist."

"Yes it would be, but let's not get the cart ahead of the horse," cautioned Camden. All present silently nodded agreement knowing the chances of finding such a passageway were not likely in their favor.

"There was a slight rap on the door and Shirley Marshal, Mr. Hicks' secretary, entered excitedly. "We have made contact and have ranger Jones on the line."

"Thank God for small favors," exclaimed Hicks as he reached for the phone. "Hicks here, are you all right?"

After a brief pause, "Good, how about Smith and the others... One dead, a number injured with broken arms or legs and some suffering from shock." Hicks repeated for the benefit of those in the room. "What is the matter with this phone connection. . . It is like you are so far away that there is a delay in the message getting to you... You noticed that as well... Ah, we'll just have to work around it. Keep someone on the phone at your end and keep this line open. Try to make people comfortable and help them stay calm... Yes you are apparently right... Let me get back to you as soon as we figure out our next move... Shirley, maintain contact through your phone with ranger Jones... don't hang up. . . keep the line open. Get a list of all the people and the extent of injuries as far as is known."

Shirley left and when Hicks heard her on the phone he put his receiver down and turned to Camden and McCoy. "That Jones is one sharp fellow. He knew the cave in was not a natural phenomena. He is a Vietnam veteran and recognized the smell of cordite afterwards. He also realized our effort to dig

The Mammoth Incident

them out was rather short lived. He doesn't have that figured out and I am not sure what to tell him... I sure don't have it figured either..."

"Let's see the ransom note again," Camden cut in. "Perhaps it will give us some idea what we are dealing with."

YOU HAVE UNTIL 18:00 HOURS TO TRANSFER $10 MILLION TO FIRST NATIONAL BANK OF PANAMA ACCOUNT #605. DO NOT ATTEMPT TO RESCUE BEFORE PAYMENT IS MADE. TO DO SO WILL RESULT IN DEATH TO ALL.

"This is ridiculous! We have one or more terrorists holding forty people captive and we don't know where they are much less who they are," exclaimed Camden.

"Whomsoever they are, they seem to be up on technology. Monitoring the entrances to the main room using TV cameras is not the run of the mill terrorist trick," replied Hicks.

"About that camera... How did that get there?" asked Camden.

"Who knows? We have used cameras in parts of the cave in the past to monitor usage and for general security. The presence of the camera probably went unnoticed or certainly unreported since we all have gotten accustomed to having them around. Who knows the one you saw could have been one of ours... Let's see, one of these documents should have the layout of the security camera system in it. If my memory serves me correctly it was installed about three years ago." Hicks turned to an adjacent shelf and proceeded to flip through some of the documents until finding the one he sought. "Yes, here it is TV Security System Mammoth Cave 1979. Well, I guess it has been longer than I thought."

"McCoy is familiar with this system, aren't you?" asked Hicks.

"I was here at the time and did supervise aspects of the operation... More from a management perspective actually... not really the on site stuff," McCoy acknowledged. "By golly, it does appear to be one of ours... At least the location is where the spec's call for one..."

"Let's see that diagram a moment... Yes, that does seem to be the location all right," affirmed Camden. " Where are the monitors for this system? Hadn't we ought to check them out?"

"Nothing to check out... Funds were never appropriated to do the job as planned in that document. All we have is a monitor at the concessionaire's office and a couple of cameras pointed at the main storeroom and one in the main foyer of the visitor center. Some other cameras were put in place but never hooked up since we couldn't get the bucks... That may be in the location where we were going to put one but I really doubt if it is one of our cameras."

Once again there was a brief tapping on the door and Shirley Marshal again stuck her head in the

The Mammoth Incident

door. "Its the President on the phone and he insist on speaking directly to you, Superintendent Hicks," she announced.

Camden and McCoy got up to leave but Hicks motioned for them to stay and picked up the receiver. "This is Superintendent Hicks...

"Yes it is rather incredible..."

"I see..."

"Yes, I understand..."

"I certainly concur and will follow your directions. We will keep your office informed of any further developments and look forward to having your representative with us.

"Good bye, Mr. President," Hicks hung up the phone and looked older than his years. A quality that Camden had not noticed before now.

"That was the President," Hicks commented knowing that it was obvious to all present already but not knowing what else to say given the circumstances. "He has indicated that we... that is the government is taking a hard line with terrorists and will not accede to their wishes under any circumstances. In other words I have been told that no ransom will be paid under any circumstances. If necessary the lives of the people trapped are forfeit if some other solution can not be found."

Hicks sat down. His action was not totally voluntary. The full force of the President's message only began to sink in when he repeated it for Camden and McCoy. His legs had weakened perceptibly.

George R. Harker

It seemed like an incredibly long time as no one spoke a word but rather stared with eyes not seeing at the chart of the cave on the wall. Actually it was only three minutes since the President's call when Shirley Marshal again entered the room. "Jones is on the line and he wants to talk with you again Superintendent Hicks"

"Very well," Hicks turned and picked up the phone, his color returning as his mind sifted focus to the tangible aspects of the business at hand rather than the abstract components.

"Yes, Jones what have you got."

"Good... Yes, by all means... Fine... No don't worry about that..."

"No, just sit tight for the time being. We are going to try to get in through one of the side entrances as soon as we can get a crew down there. It shouldn't take more than a few hours. Better tell the folks it will be longer so they don't panic if it takes a little longer than we expect," Hicks said. "Fine, sounds like you have things well under control."

"Well that is good news. It seems the dust has settled both figuratively and actually. Among the group was a couple of nurses and a paramedic. They have given first aid to those that needed it. Our crews must have found the break in the power line. They have lights again and that seems to be helping everyone a great deal. Things may be going our way, at least a little. It seems one of the Civil Defense stashes of food, medicine, and blankets was just off

The Mammoth Incident

the section of the corridor in which they are trapped. Good old Jones was a little fearful about opening them since this wasn't a nuclear attack... He always has been one to go by the book... I think I convinced him that his actions were in accord with Park Service policy." Camden and McCoy were hard pressed to contain themselves when they heard this understatement from Hicks.

Chapter Seven

Two Hours Later

The plan was simple enough. They would enter the cut off section of the main cave through the side entrance found by Mitchel in his review of the old survey. Make contact with Smith and Jones and then take everyone out without the terrorist being any the wiser. With a plan so simple and straightforward Camden wanted to know why the hair on the back of his neck chose this moment to achieve a position different than its usual prone posture to which he was more accustomed.

Camden and Riley entered the cave via the elevator to the middle level. Walking through the strangely empty dining area they continued down the main passageway just as hundreds of thousands of cave visitors had done over the years. About half-way down the passageway Riley vaulted over the side rail and started to climb the rock face stepping on foot holds that Camden could not yet see. Within seconds Riley made the ledge. About six feet from the access point to the ledge a large fissure became apparent to Camden. From Camden's position it appeared like a vee-shaped cut, perhaps eight feet tall. About three feet across at the top and tapering to nothing at the ledge. Riley wedged a foot into the vee and slid in sideways. Camden lit his carbide lantern and proceeded to follow the agile Mr. Riley.

Surprisingly Camden found he was able to locate the hand and toe holds that Riley used, or at

The Mammoth Incident

least a reasonable facsimile, for he gained the ledge and the vee in no time at all. Wedging sideways into the vee was not all that difficult either for one only had to wiggle about twenty feet before it opened into a relatively large passageway which approximately paralleled the main passageway they had just left.

If he understood correctly this passage would continue on for a couple of hundred feet and end in a breakdown. A pile of rocks representing the roof of that portion of the cave thousands of years ago. At the top of the rock pile was another passageway one could crawl through. This in turn ran diagonally across and above the passageway where the group was trapped. A vertical chimney would drop them down to the level of the main cave and another vee shaped opening similar to that which they had entered to get to this point would take them into the main cave just above the area where the civil defense supplies were stored.

The passageway they were in could not be totally discerned with the light of their carbide lamps. Its size was such that the lanterns didn't provide sufficient luminescence. Walking slightly behind and to the left of Riley, Camden wondered if the injured would be able to traverse the passageways even with assistance. He concluded he would just have to cross that bridge when he got to it. And the way things were going that would be more than twenty to thirty minutes at best.

Camden caught a glimpse of the object in the

perimeter of the lighted area ahead just before it hit him. He had instinctively ducked and few could move faster when confronted with situations demanding a fast response. Nevertheless the object caught Camden right in the mouth.

Camden fell backward to the ground. His helmet with carbide light attached rolled off and clattered to a stop out of arms reach. The lamp flickered and went out.

Riley turned and looked in disbelief at Camden nearly prone on the cave floor.

Camden couldn't understand why his jaw didn't hurt. In fact, he couldn't understand why nothing hurt at all. In the past he had often evaded blows to the head and face with various degrees of success. But never in his conscious memory had he taken a direct hit to the mouth without pain, usually a rather excruciating pain. If not felt initially in the fury of the moment it was always there when that moment had passed. This time there was no pain and the moment had clearly passed.

"Perhaps I'm dead and this is how it feels," reflected Camden. Slowly he pulled himself up to a sitting position. Having done so he became aware of Riley laughing hysterically.

"I don't think I have ever seen someone move so fast in my life," said Riley with tears forming in his eyes reflecting the intensity of the amusement. "And just to get out of the way of a little old bat."

Camden's grin turned to laughter as he too

The Mammoth Incident

realized what had happened. A wayward bat had triggered the conditioned reflexes developed in many hours of hand to hand combat training. His fall to the ground was not the result of a bone crushing impact to the jaw, but the avoidance reaction to an almost unseen bat.

"I though bats were supposed to avoid hitting things with that radar they got," Camden quipped.

"Maybe he though you were another bat and was trying to mate," was Riley's comeback.

Camden was not sure if he was tasting bat fur or if his taste buds and mind were playing tricks on him. Time was wasting and the time for levity would come later when the hostages were released. Riley recovered and lighted the carbide and the two headed for the breakdown up ahead. Camden keeping a sharper lookout for bats than before. None were sighted, however.

The breakdown was different than Camden had imagined. It consisted of a pile of large rocks of various sizes slanting at a rather abrupt angle to just below the roof line of the cave. Or so Camden perceived it since the light of both beams was insufficient to actually illuminate the ceiling. Instead the rock pile just continued in the general direction of the ceiling off through the darkness that enveloped them.

The rock pile appeared to be relatively unstable. Indeed, the surface rocks were resting where the force of gravity had been overcome by the friction of rock rolling on rock as it moved down the incline. In some cases this friction grip was just slightly stronger than the grip of gravity and the intrusion of a force from a human foot or hand seeking a hold was enough to tip the scales to gravity. Rocks, so nudged, would move imperceptibly at first and then break loose to roll or slide down the incline until a larger force such as another rock countered to offset gravity again. While this struggle had been going on for eons it was apparent that gravity would ultimately prevail. It was just a matter of time.

Riley suggested they move up the rock pile in close proximity to one another. In so doing any rocks knocked loose would fall harmlessly down the slope below them. Camden agreed with the logic of the idea and they started upward.

Every now and again a rock would yield to gravity and tumble down crashing into the darkness. Most of the tumbling and crashing could be attributed to the actions of the two men. Occasionally a rumble would emanate from some other section of the breakdown indicating that the forces of nature were still at work even in this subterranean environment.

A rock about the size of a grapefruit bounced past Camden as he moved less than a few feet behind Riley. Then before he fully comprehended its passage another one of slightly larger size bounced by on the other side. The actual size of the rocks Camden could not know for they were only slightly in his carbide's field of illumination. The relative intensity of the

The Mammoth Incident

sound as rock hit rock suggested the difference in size. Mixed in was the sound of numerous smaller rocks cascading down the pile; the inevitable chain reaction of one rock hitting another and then another. Each rock dislodged another two in a sort of chain reaction.

About the time Camden realized these rocks were not dislodged by his partner, it was over. A boulder about three feet across caught Riley in the chest as it rebounded down the slope from somewhere above. The impact rolled Riley's body backward and down the hill catching Camden as it went.

Whether the crushed chest or the broken neck killed Riley might not be a mute point to the coroner, but it was to Camden. He lay still, pinned by the grotesque form which moments before had been a warm caring person and by bits of debris knocked lose from higher up the slope. Too stunned to move and constrained by the body over him and the rocks around him, Camden gazed at the dust swirling in the beams of light shining upward from the two carbide lamps. For some unknown reason they had not been snuffed out.

Camden was oblivious to everything as he gazed at the dancing particles of dust or at any rate almost oblivious. At first he thought it was the clatter of rocks still settling from the impact of those that had just swept by. Without moving his head he realized that the sounds where coming from up the slope and not from below. Another rock fall? Then a few more seconds then another small rock tumbled by off to his left about 30 feet. Did the initial sound seem closer or was that his imagination? Camden lay motionless and directed all his energy to his ears, not realizing he only had to move his head to get a better fix on the source of the sound.

There it was again and this time there could be no doubt the sound of dislodged rocks was getting closer, as were the rocks themselves as they rolled down the hillside. Just as Camden decided it was time to get moving, a light from a third carbide lantern flashed across his face and moved to rest on the corpse.

Camden froze nearly as motionless as the very rocks whose company he kept. The light returned and briefly scanned over his body and then darted off in the direction from which they had come minutes before.

From the corner of his eye Camden could detect a human form as it moved down the rock pile dislodging a small boulder every now and again to crash down the hillside. While it seemed like an eternity it was only minutes before the form reached the bottom of the breakdown and headed off down the passage retracing the steps of Camden and Riley.

Camden breathed deeply in relief and to see if everything was still functioning internally. Nothing seemed to indicate anything unusual. Lungs and rib cage seemed to be functioning as intended. Camden pulled one arm free then the other, doing so ever so gently to avoid dislodging any rocks. He was only

The Mammoth Incident

partly successful as a small one rolled down the slope. To Camden it seemed like its impact against other rocks was similar to sticks of dynamite going off. Actually, to the objective observer, it was hardly noticeable.

Camden checked to see if the third carbide was still visible. It was not. He eased the broken body of Riley off of his and stood up. To his surprise nothing seemed broken or even sprained. He would have a few bruises in the morning to be sure.

Camden pondered his situation and decided his best option was to pursue the human form which seemed to be retracing his route. That form was the most tangible link to the terrorists, whomever they might be. Without further reflection he eased down the slope as carefully as he could and proceeded at a run in an effort to catch the form. After a short distance Camden realized he best slow down or he might miss the turn and the vee that was the only exit he knew out of this portion of the cave. His decision was made at the opportune time for just a few feet further was the outcrop which marked the way back. On the run he undoubtedly would have shot right past it without knowing it.

He took off his helmet and peered into the passageway looking for the light of the third carbide. He could not be certain if he saw a fleeting ray of light or not. In any event the other human was well into the passage and not right there confronting him face to face. Camden was relieved to find that was the case.

Instinctively Camden worked his way through the passage and out on to the ledge. Down the passageway toward the elevators where he had entered only a little more than an hour before he could detect the faint sound of someone running. Then another sound, that of a metal door closing against its door frame.

Camden jumped from the ledge to the uneven cave floor below and rolled on his thigh rather than take the full force on his ankles. A rather fortuitous decision given the way one foot was deflected by the uneven rock surface. He pulled himself to his feet and ran toward the elevators. On the way he leaped the path rail without so much as losing stride.

At the elevators he spun around to find two steel doors. One heading away from the lobby, perhaps into another section of cave, Camden had no idea. The other was at the top of a short set of stairs and clearly marked exit. Camden decided on the latter and bounded up the steps. The door yielded to his pull and he pushed through to find a spiraling staircase of metal and concrete which looked to be as old as the cave itself. He started to climb taking three steps at a time. Part way up he heard the metallic click of a steel door against a door frame. The keeper on the door below him had just pulled shut. Another two steps and he heard the metallic click of another steel door only this time the sound came from above.

Camden renewed his effort to close the

The Mammoth Incident

distance. Within another minute he was at the top of the stairwell. He hit the panic bar on the door and bolted outward. The mid-afternoon sun was blinding to eyes still accustomed to illumination by carbide lantern. Camden actually staggered backwards in his momentary disorientation. Peering between his cupped hands he fought to ascertain where he was and more importantly where the fleeing figure had gone.

The first question was quickly laid aside when he recognized the parking lot in front of him as the one just south of the main visitor center, essentially the back of the building he had entered earlier to get into the cave. The solution to the second question was more elusive.

His eyes adjusting to the light, Camden noted a small Toyota easing into a parking space about thirty feet from him. At the far end of the lot he caught a brief glimpse of a Chevy as it pulled onto the access road and disappeared behind some white pine plantings placed by a landscape architect intent on shielding the view of the parking lot from the road. The placement was particularly effective even from this angle and Camden would attest to that if anyone asked. No one would ask.

Instinctively Camden knew the person he sought was in that Chevy. He approached the driver of the Toyota, a middle aged woman who looked like a school teacher. As she fumbled with the keys in the process of locking the car, Camden took them from her hand, said something about "official business" and eased by her into the car without a moment's hesitation. The car sprung to life in an instant. It lurched backward with intermittent stops about twenty feet until Camden realized he hadn't taken off the emergency brake. Another lurch and the squeal of tires as Camden popped the clutch on the revving motor and the Toyota was well underway.

Meanwhile the bewildered woman stood motionless where Camden had left her. Her wondering eyes betrayed a mind trying to comprehend what was happening. A moment later she started to step forward lifting an arm pointing in the direction of her departing Toyota. Sensing the total futility of her efforts she dropped her arm, shrugged her shoulders, and started to sob to herself as tires screeched in the distance.

Chapter Eight

Camden forced the Toyota into third gear at the same time pushing the accelerator to the floor. The car lurched, seemed to dig in and start to accelerate at a faster rate than it had before. Of course that was exactly what Camden had in mind. Without increased speed the car ahead would leave him with little more than exhaust fumes.

Rounding the next curve Camden noticed the blue Chevy he had been pursuing with such diligence pulled to the side of the road and two figures moving down the slope to a boat waiting at the shoreline. Both climbed aboard the bow which had been nudged into the bank to facilitate the collection of passengers. The boat operator quickly threw the powerful inboard-outboard into full reverse pulling the craft from the shore as Camden braked to a halt alongside the Chevy.

A sense of frustration started to overcome Camden as he looked out across the lake as the boat reached planing speed and glided away leaving only a silver wake lapping against the shore, not more than thirty feet from where he stood. The range to the boat was already too great for pistol fire, and he certainly wasn't about to swim after them. Camden turned and walked back to the Toyota. Before he could get in he noticed another vehicle moving down the highway towing a boat trailer.

The van contained a group of teenagers heading to the reservoir for an afternoon of water skiing behind their father's rather souped up ski boat.

George R. Harker

Camden did look rather officious in his National Park Service uniform even if it was a little wrinkled. The youths did not have any reason to doubt that this man in uniform was working in some official capacity even if they had never encountered someone this far from the launching ramp at the park.

"May I see your driver's license and boat registration?" Camden inquired.

"We haven't done anything! What's the problem? We weren't speeding," asserted the youth driving the van as he reached for his billfold.

"No problem, just a routine safety check. We just want to be sure your boat is in good working order and in accord with Coast Guard safety regulations. Hop out and let's see those life jackets and fire extinguishers. Won't take a minute and you can be on you way," Camden remarked in as a matter of fact manner as he could muster given the nature of his true intentions.

Surprisingly the young man complied and walked with Camden to the boat. "Nice piece of equipment you've got here. I'll bet a boat like this takes a lot of preparation before launching?" intimated Camden.

"Na, just have to drop it in the water and flip the ignition switch. Got it all fueled up and ready to go before we left the house," volunteered the youngest looking of the three.

"Here are the life jackets and the fire extinguisher is right under the dash to the left," noted

The Mammoth Incident

the van driver. "Can we go now?"

"Fine, just a couple more things and you will qualify for the safety sticker. Let's check out these tie down straps. Lots of people overlook these and they can get pretty frayed without being noticed. This will only take another minute or two and it may prevent you losing your boat on some hill when you least expect it. Let's take the tension off and see what we've got," Camden instructed.

The boys looked intently as Camden released the tension on the tie down and proceeded to study the strap with a jaundiced eye. "Check that other side, guys. I'll tell you what to look for." As the young men moved to the opposite side of the boat to release the other tie down, Camden moved forward to "check" the bow connection. Releasing this he started to move to join the boys at the remaining tie down. Before moving more than a few feet he deliberately paused, as the boys looked up in awareness Camden directed the older youth to check the brake light on the trailer while Camden activated the brakes in the van.

Camden slid into the vinyl bucket seat and hit the brake. At the same instant he flipped the ignition key and gave it gas. The van sprang to life with not so much as a cough and Camden knew his luck was changing. He dropped the shift lever into drive and was thirty feet down the road before the youths realized what had happened. When the distance seemed adequate to prevent the boys from closing quickly, Camden headed the van and trailer directly toward the lake. There wasn't time for a more conventional launch.

Slowing the van to a speed approaching that of a jogger, Camden stepped out the door, pivoted and faced the boat as it rolled by. At what appeared to be the last second Camden grabbed the side of the boat and pulled himself into the cockpit. Although brush and debris worked against the forward progress of the van its sheer mass and momentum carried it into the water and out from the shore.

The van floated, suggesting a variation of an amphibious houseboat, and then started to sink. Meanwhile the trailer had dropped below the surface leaving Camden and the boat floating toward the still sinking van.

Camden turned the ignition switch and hoped the kids knew what they were talking about when they said it was ready to go. He was not disappointed. The modified 455 erupted with a barely muffled explosion and Camden knew he was in business. As he moved the throttle forward, the boat leaped to plane and moved on down the lake.

On shore three exhausted and disbelieving boys looked at the sinking van then at each other. "How will you ever explain this to dad," conjectured the youngest of the three.

"Do you think we passed the safety check?" jested the middle one.

Camden peered intently at the horizon trying to be sure he still had the fleeting runabout in sight.

The Mammoth Incident

Believing he did, the next question was whether he was gaining on it. Although the answer seemed to be an unqualified yes, the time delay had given a considerable advantage to the fleeing craft.

Flat out the ski boat skipped over the water like a flat stone. It seemed to leap from point to point just barely keeping the prop in the water.

Up ahead Camden saw the minute speck growing as the distance closed. Just as the spot began to take on characteristics of a boat it abruptly turned leeward and rounded a point of rock and shore protruding into the lake. Camden altered course to turn the transverse angle that would close the gap even quicker than through sheer use of speed. The strategy was working. The distance between the crafts or at least where the crafts would have been had not one been obscured by the rocky outcrop was diminishing rapidly.

Camden pitched forward with a force that took him right over the low windscreen of the ski-boat. Continuing in a series of uncontrolled somersaults Camden covered the front deck of an almost stationary speed boat at about the same velocity that the craft had attained only a brief moment earlier.

The water was refreshingly cool as Camden fought to re-orient his aching body at the same time he fought to clear the water from his nose and mouth. A breath of air in the near future was deemed essential, if not consciously known to Camden, it was obvious to his unconscious mind and every other component of his being concerned with survival.

This time the shock to the senses was as close to a false alarm as is possible in such a situation. For as Camden straightened up, he found his feet firmly planted on a sand and rock base only three feet below the surface. The boat that had moments before skimmed the surface was just to his right with small waves lapping over the gunnels as the 455 horses gave one last cough as water poured into the dual carburetors.

About fifteen feet aft of the sinking craft bits of fiberglass hull, a twisted rudder and unidentifiable components of a lower unit protruded briefly through an undulating oil slick. Camden found that the sand and rock bottom sloped upward to the very spot where the debris lay. The causal aspects of the other crafts earlier maneuvering became painfully apparent to Camden. A rocky shoal extended off the point and was known to any local boater. Unfortunately, Camden was not a local.

Chapter Nine

Twenty Four Hours Later

"We have received another ransom note," explained Hicks. "They indicate one person will die every twenty four hours until their demands are met. Apparently they believe both Riley and Camden were killed at the breakdown and that further efforts to reach the trapped people will result in similar losses."

"How could they know of any losses? We have not released any information to the press and only four of us knew of the attempt, much less the outcome," McCoy noted.

"The terrorist did know we were coming because whoever was at the breakdown was prepared and waiting for our arrival. But who did know besides the three of us excluding Riley for the moment? Weren't Smith and Jones advised about our plans?"

"Yes they were told by me on the phone. I don't believe anyone else was on that line. Shirley was the only other person with access to the line in the outer office.

*****

As the elevator descended Camden wondered why he was going again into the cave. He kept telling himself that the plan made sense before, therefore it still ought to make sense now. True, the element of surprise and secrecy might not be there, but then it wasn't there before and Riley had died for that. But maybe, just maybe the element of surprise might be there. Perhaps it was more so than before. This time Smith and Jones did not know they were coming. Instead they had been told about the ransom demands and to sit tight, that efforts to make communications with the terrorist would continue with no further effort to rescue them for the time being. Furthermore, Camden was mentally and physically prepared for anything. He had thought he was so prepared in his last trip but in truth the events encountered far exceeded his expectations. They were well beyond the range he had mentally prepared for. This time would be different.

In terms of physical preparation he had brought along his Remington 32 caliber automatic complete with a silencer. This he wore under his jacket in a chest holster. He had never really used the silencer before on a mission since it was a pain to carry and not of any real utility. If things got to a point where someone had to be shot, it didn't much matter if someone heard it or not as far as he was concerned. In his years with the force the few times he had fired his weapon on the job the results had fatal consequences and no particular difficulties arose over the noise pollution associated with the "incidents." Actually, he hadn't changed his mind about the philosophical aspects of the question of using a silencer or not. It was quite simply a practical consideration in deference to his own ears. Blasting away in the confines of a cave would have rather

The Mammoth Incident

definite effects on his ear drums as the sound of the muzzle blast reverberated in such a confined space. Camden did not want to face retirement with a substantial hearing loss if it could be reasonably avoided. The use of the silencer seemed a reasonable solution to the problem.

Riding down the elevator with Camden was Milly Malone. She was a seasoned spelunker at 29 even if only with the park service for three years as a seasonal ranger. Camden was still amused over the introduction of the previous hour. He thought Hicks had said "Wily " Malone and was a bit taken aback when Wily removed his helmet in the briefing room to release dark hair which cascaded to her shoulders before being subdued into a pony tail and wrapped into a tight bun and returned to a place under her helmet.

Hicks, noting Camden's astonishment, smiled and assured Camden that she was one of the best spelunkers in the service.

Camden had no basis on which to gauge her spelunking skills but if appearance had any bearing then he had no doubts she was right up there with the best. Actually, he didn't attempt to make any comparisons. He would judge a woman's looks or ability by his own standards as the opportunities arose. He could judge her beauty easily enough on the information he had available at the moment and the rest would follow. Past experience with Hicks' observations supported the likelihood that she was indeed as skilled a spelunker as she was pleasant to look at. Camden was pleased with that possibility. He did not care for good looking woman with empty heads or flabby midriffs. Milly, actually Millisa Jane Malone had neither.

Camden could not help but glance to the steel door and the staircase as he stepped from the elevator. He thought he felt a slight twinge in the calf muscles of his legs. Perhaps his subconscious was just recalling the events of yesterday. He moved on down the corridor with Milly close at hand. Neither spoke. Milly had been briefed on the events of the previous day and there was little more to do but get on with it.

Their measured strides quickly took them down the passageway to the spot on the walkway across from the ledge. Camden stopped long enough to light his carbide lamp and proceeded up the hand holds to the ledge. After a pause to listen at the vee and the scan of his light to further check, he pulled his automatic and lead with that hand into the crevasse. Milly was at his side in a moment and they both pressed through to the larger passage on the other end.

Before emerging from the opening Camden removed his helmet and holding it at arms length shined the light in a 180 degree sweep from one side to the other. His second hand, bearing the automatic, followed with the hammer cocked and ready to respond to the muzzle flash he hoped to provoke. There was no flash or so much as a sound. Camden

The Mammoth Incident

breathed easier and moved from the vee into the opening still keeping the lamp well ahead. In spite of the directional nature of the beam the two were faintly lit as they edged forward.

Camden felt like a sitting duck even though he had had Milly douse her light. He knew that in the cave even a few stray light rays would be enough to provide a target for a waiting gunman. His hope was that the gunman would aim for some point just below the lantern trying for a killing head shot before realizing that the head was some two feet removed from its usual location within the helmet. That oversight and the muzzle flash was what Camden was counting on to give him the edge he did not feel he had at the moment.

Nothing happened. Moving down the passageway Camden eased the action of the automatic to safety and placed the weapon back in his shoulder holster. He placed his helmet and lantern back on his head and motioned for Milly to do the same.

"I didn't really think they would be on to us this time. If they were, this would have been a very logical place to take us out. Between here and breakdown is a possibility, but not likely... If we keep moving we wouldn't be as good a target," Camden told Milly in a tone of voice above a whisper but not quite a normal conversational level.

"Here is where I wrestled with that bat," smiled Camden as they moved past some disturbed soil and gravel in the pathway.

"Must have been a large one to knock you down," returned Milly with a warm smile.

"Indeed... had a six foot wingspan. . . large pointed teeth... quite a frightful thing."

Up ahead the breakdown loomed up in the farther reaches of their carbides' beams. Camden motioned to Milly to douse her light, which she did quickly. He slipped off his carbide and helmet with one hand as he slipped his other into his shoulder holster.

"Wait here, let me check out ahead."

Camden moved to the base of the breakdown prepared for the muzzle flash or falling rock which never came. He paused and waited. Nothing happened. Feeling his earlier combination of premonition and logic was correct he shone his lantern in Milly's direction and motioned for her to come over to him.

They stood at the base of the breakdown. In unison they swept the beams back and forth across the rock pile straining their eyes to detect even the slightest movement. But none was seen. One of the two beams returned to the passed over body of Riley and lingered. The second beam, as if noticing the first, returned and also paused.

"There wasn't time to do anything but leave him... Perhaps later when we have this place secured..."

"I understand... It just isn't the same when you actually see someone you know dead. I mean I just

The Mammoth Incident

didn't expect it to be like this... It is so gruesome."

"Violent death usually is... particularly when not expected," Camden took Milly's hand in his and squeezed it gently. In a warm soft voice, "It was quick, he did not feel any pain... if that is any consolation." Moving the beam to the top of the breakdown. "I would feel a lot better if we controlled the high ground. Hold on to my shirt tail and let us get to the top of this rock pile before someone comes along."

The climb was not that difficult if you could get used to the sound of small boulders and large rocks rolling into the darkness to dislodge other rocks and boulders which in turn bounded off. At the top Camden found the opening they were looking for and eased through.

Although he was expecting a moderate sized passageway he was pleasantly surprised to find one with a five foot ceiling. He could walk upright if he just stooped over a bit. Just inside the opening from the breakdown the passageway flared to a generous four feet before tapering down to a two foot passageway about eight feet from where they had entered. The floor of the chamber was interesting in its own right. It was covered by a fine sand with only an occasional fine pebble mixed in. It was also dry, or at least dryer than any cave this far below the surface had a right to be.

Scanning his beam around the chamber Camden could discern the impressions of a small ribbed boot generally in the portion of the passage closest to the way he had entered. In many places the impression of one print overlapped and distorted the impressions of others. Were these the tracks of Riley's killer? Camden was certain that they were and made a mental note of one of the better impressions. He gauged the size against his own palm for future reference. This was a crude but effective way of calibrating his memory.

"It's clear, who ever was here before is not here now," Camden said reassuringly as he offered Milly a hand and pulled her into the chamber. "You are trembling."

"I know, I just didn't expect it to be like this... Seeing Riley lying there... I'm sorry Mick... I'll be all right... Just give me a couple of minutes to pull myself together," came the measured response of a visibly shaken Milly. Her grip on Camden's hand had become a clutching of his outstretched arm.

Camden instinctively knew what she needed. Without thinking he drew her to his body and held her tight. He caressed her head and neck gently until the trembling subsided. She held her chin tucked against his chest.

A few minutes passed in the total silence of the underground marred only by an occasional muffled sob and the rhythmic sound of conscious breathing.

Turning to face Camden, Milly whispered, "Thank you. I will be all right now I just needed to be held." She kissed him gently on the lips. Not satisfied

The Mammoth Incident

that her action was sufficient acknowledgement of her gratitude or confused by the change in her emotions welling up within her she sought his lips again. The intensity of her embrace evoked a mutually intense feeling of desire within Camden. His hands moved gently over her body and glided within her shirt to feel the warmth of her breast. Simultaneously her hands had unbuttoned his shirt and found his chest. She moved from his mouth to the small of his neck nibbling and kissing gently as she went. Before much more could elapse, an unspoken time out was signaled and acknowledged by both with signals unheard and unseen but nevertheless clearly communicated as they have been through the ages. Whatever barriers clothes might create were eliminated by their complete removal and placement on the sandy cave floor as the next best thing to a mattress of a more suitable material.

Camden lay flat on his back as the caressing kisses resumed where they had left off. A flick of the tongue on the left nipple and then a soft touch of lips and tongue just below the rib cage. Her hand glided over his hip and inside his thigh. She ran her lips and tongue from tip to bottom and back again. Her hair sent shivers of sensation through his body as it brushed about in a pattern that was not accidental.

To no avail he tried to decide which sensation was the most delectable. Was it the sense of touch as she caressed his body? Was it the sound of lips and tongue and labored breathing? Or was it the soft shape of the female form draped over him lit by the subdued reflection of the carbide lamps on the cave walls? He could not say, for as experienced in the ways of making love as he was, he had never experienced anything quite like this.

His right hand slid down and over the curved contour of her shapely behind and between her yielding thighs. The folds within were warm and moist with expectation. A few caresses to enhance that expectation and the shadowed forms of soft curves and rounded hillocks began to change shape. That which had been the inner-facing of two adjacent thighs shifted to encompass his body where before nothing but his hand had been between. Pushed back slightly to meet the descending vee created by the confluence of two soft thighs, his member told of the moist warmth as it was slowly engulfed. Immersed to the hilt and then nearly released it stiffened further in anticipation.

Camden gazed upward at the pendulous breasts rising and falling with each penetration. His hands clasped the soft skin of her waist and then slid upward to gently compress the pulsating breasts. Compressing them slightly he ran his finger over and around the stiffened and erect nipples. A gasp of pleasure issued from the bowed body over him as the hair on the tossed back head danced in the carbide light.

Then forward came the breasts with the body following respectively behind to be compressed against

The Mammoth Incident

his chest as more kisses and caresses engulfed him. He brushed the fingernails of both hands down the curve of her back and felt the convulsive tremors of orgasmic aftershocks pulse through her. After a few moments she returned to an upright configuration with her head thrown back and her arms braced against his chest and began to undulate her pelvis on his lap. Her pubic hairs commingling with his as the gyrations increased in intensity and frenzy. The sensations were such that it seemed certain that at any moment the cosmic flow would burst forth. And then as rapidly as it began it was over, the murmurs and gasp for air took on a more subdued level as the quivering form dropped again to cover his outstretched form. Orgasmic aftershocks surged through her warm body at intermittent intervals as he held her close.

Without breaking the union the two rolled over to begin again. Slipping his arms under her shoulders he squeezed her flattened breast tightly to his chest. With slowly increasing frequency he thrust deeply and then fell back nearly, but not quite releasing the captured organ's head from the warm moist grip of its captor.

With each thrust he felt the epicenter of the universe move closer to the tip of his phallic probe. And then with shorter intervals between breaths he knew the focus of the universe was there but would not stay as it surged onward and outward to be experienced briefly at another time and place.

The intensity of the orgasmic release was enhanced by the strange prickly feeling that Camden could feel in the small of his back. As near as he could determine he first became aware of it at the moment of release. Yet something told him it had been there just prior to release and had actually contributed. Now he lay limp on the soft cushion of the radiant form that still trembled below him from an occasional, although less frequent, aftershock of pleasure. No, he was not imagining things he felt it again. Whatever it was it was moving across his back. With that realization his body shuddered and shifted from total relaxation to tension accompanied by goose bumps and a sort of tingly sensation. Camden slowly reached to the area where the sensations most recently originated and whisked the area clear with the motion of his hand. Out of the corner of his eye he observed an insect like creature flutter to the ground in the shadows of the carbide lantern. Camden had never seen a cave cricket before, much less experienced one close up. He was not sure he really relished the opportunity and deep in his heart felt he would have been no worse for wear if he had not encountered one at this particular time.

Chapter Ten

Camden felt his sexual desires diminished considerably quicker than usual as he contemplated the cave cricket. The collapse of his sexual appetite was not only figurative but literal. It was so much so that a still to be fully satiated Milly inquired as to the difficulty.

Camden's explanation only succeeded in making both aware of a coolness in the cave which in turn moved them to dress and remember why they had come.

Groping for his left shoe Camden felt a round metallic object protruding from the sand. Recognizing it by touch as a pendant he quickly handed it to Milly.

"What is this," she asked sarcastically," a token of appreciation."

"No, what are you talking about? It is yours, is it not? I just found it where you dropped it."

"I wish it were mine but I don't have the bucks for a medallion with a price tag like that," handing the piece back to Camden.

Holding the pendant under the light of the carbide, Camden realized what Milly was talking about. The piece was a Krugerrand with a gold band around it to hold it securely in place. A gold chain passed through an eyelet at the top of the band. It appeared that the clasp at one end was broken and the short piece of a secondary safety chain was also broken. The previous owner had not parted with the piece knowingly, based on the evidence in hand.

Camden dropped it into his shirt pocket, "The

owner may be the one responsible for Riley's death. Let us keep this to ourselves for the time being."

Milly understood and shook her head in agreement. The two finished dressing and picked up their equipment. Moving to the back of the chamber they eased sideways into the crack that would take them to the vertical chimney that would return them to the level of the cave they sought.

The slight pressure of the medallion in Camden's pocket served to heighten his awareness to every sound in the cave. His hand moved toward the shoulder holster on more than one occasion before the conscious mind caught hold and stopped the unconscious act in progress.

The chimney was smaller than the old maps seemed to suggest. Perhaps Camden was bigger than the previous explorer of the passage. In any event movement down the chimney would require that he place his back against one side of the crevice and wedge his feet against the opposite side with his legs bent and under tension to keep from dropping abruptly to the bottom. Camden felt strangely vulnerable in this position as he edged downward a few inches at a time.

In what seemed like hours, but was actually only a few minutes of intense concentration, Camden found himself at the bottom of the chimney. Here he found the lateral passage he sought. Just big enough to maneuver around in if one was content with the crouching position which had to be assumed to fit.

The Mammoth Incident

Given he didn't have any choice Camden decided it could be far worse and accepted the situation as he found it.

Milly scrambled down the chimney in a flash, or so it seemed to Camden. In fact she was quicker than Camden but not quite to the degree that he imagined.

"If I understand the maps correctly, the main chamber is about fifty feet down this passage. It should open out just above and behind the civil defense supplies stacked in this side pocket," Camden pointed to a xerox copy of an old map. "Let's ease up on them and see what is going on rather than just walk in unannounced."

Milly acknowledged her acceptance of Camden's suggestion and they proceeded on hands and knees down the passage.

The view of the main chamber was limited by rock outcroppings. Camden figured he could only see about a third, if that much of the main grotto. In the area he could see, he observed people clustered together in small groups conversing and generally passing the time. In another portion of the cave just visible to him he saw a form draped by a khaki blanket. He presumed this was the fatality he had heard about earlier.

One individual in a ranger uniform circulated from group to group. Bits of laughter could be heard from the groups so visited. It was not the boisterous laughter of a good party but rather the forced laughter of people in a stressed situation trying to make the best of it.

Camden thought it was indeed fortunate that the electric lines supplying the cave lights had stayed up. He could not imagine the gravity of the situation if the tour group had been plunged into total darkness. For even with the lights there was a sense of doom that seemed to envelop the group below. Indeed it seemed to be permeating the very crawl space from which he and Milly quietly observed.

Camden contemplated the situation and wondered how he could get the attention of one of the rangers without revealing his presence to the entire group. He wasn't sure why he didn't want to reveal their presence to the group, but something a kin to a sixth sense that had kept him out of trouble in the past was sending a message he was not inclined to ignore.

It seemed like hours when in fact it had been about an hour and a half when a young boy came poking around the supplies more out of a sense of boredom than any need for what the cache might contain. That is not to say thoughts of a nice peanut butter and jelly sandwich were not in the youth's head.

"Psst"

The youth jumped somewhat startled but not panicked.

"Up here above you... don't look up and keep your voice down. We don't want anyone to know we are here," whispered Camden. The youth involuntarily

The Mammoth Incident

glanced up to where Camden peered over the ledge. When his gaze met Camden's he smiled. Camden's answering smile put both of them at ease. The boy went back to poking around the supplies. "After a while and in a manner that wouldn't attract attention would you ask one of the rangers to come over. Explain that we don't want people to know we are here just yet," Camden directed in his most low keyed yet distinctively authoritative way.

The sense of urgency and a need for complicity was not lost on the youth who said "Yes sir, I'll get the ranger... How did you get here?"

"No time for explanations now. Will you let me tell you later?" Camden acknowledged.

The youth nodded and casually walked back into the main portion of the cave. Camden watched him mingle with a group and then taking the ranger aside appeared to be looking in Camden's direction. A few moments later the ranger was poking around the civil defense supplies apparently looking for something.

"Smith, is that you?" inquired Camden.

"No, I'm Jones," came the terse but controlled reply without Jones even looking up. "Who are you and what is the plan?"

"My name is Camden. Mick Camden. Milly Malone is here with me. We came to try and get you people out of here through a little known side passage without the terrorist being any the wiser," Camden explained.

"Great concept, but I doubt it will work. We have some injured here that can only go out on a stretcher. What about them?" asked Jones.

"A good question, but let's get those that are able out of here and reduce the exposure by that amount and maybe we can find some other way to save the rest," Camden responded.

"There may be another problem," indicated Jones.

"What would that be?" asked Camden.

"Have you been watching us on the remote TV camera system?"

"No, what are you talking about?"

"Just what I feared. Every now and then the remote cameras sweep across the area. I didn't know what it was at first, then I finally figured out what the very faint whine was which I kept hearing now and then. Someone is activating the remote TV cameras in here and if it isn't you and the Park Service I suspect the operator is working for the opposition," Jones explained in subdued tones that only Camden and Milly could hear.

Camden recalled his earlier experience with the TV camera and decided to store this tidbit for further consideration. "We need to find some way to disable those cameras. I am beginning to think this cave is wired in ways we have yet to know."

"I note you didn't tell us you were coming this time," remarked Jones.

"Given the reception we got the last time it

The Mammoth Incident

seemed better to surprise you. At least this way we weren't surprised."

Camden was getting a feeling in the pit of the stomach that did not sit well with him. It was the involuntary sign that things were not going the way he had it planned. This wouldn't have bothered him a great deal if he could have dismissed his anxiety with good rational explanations and a scenario that sounded feasible. The trouble was he couldn't come up with anything that seemed remotely plausible. Here he was talking to one of the trapped victims with his back to an escape passage that most could master with a bit of effort and yet he knew that further efforts along that line were doomed to futility.

It seemed that at best all he had was a direct link to the victims if a runner was willing to make the trek. Small consolation given the death of Riley. Pitifully short of the quick solution envisioned when he first came up with the idea of pulling the captives out a side entrance and leaving the captors with an empty cave. There was no point in dwelling on it further. The link was established and would be useful in any event. Time was the crucial consideration and Camden knew he had to get back topside and try a different tack. What that might be he couldn't say. He hoped some great idea would be revealed soon. The feeling in the pit of his stomach was growing.

"If the cave is being monitored we can't take people out without them being missed and that is bound to provoke the terrorist. It is safer if we just sit tight for a few more hours. What do you think, Jones? Have you got the supplies you need to hang in there for a few more hours?" asked Camden.

"If it is just a few more hours I think we can make it. There are a few things we could use. Some medical supplies and the water here is terrible. Any possibility of getting some in here that is a little more potable?" Jones queried.

"I'll see what I can do."

"What do you want me to do?" asked Milly who had been silent to this point.

"I don't know, got any suggestions?" Camden responded. "I am a bit short on ideas and open to suggestions."

"Let me stay and help Jones. I could start briefing these people on some caving techniques so when the time comes to go for it they will know what to do. . . At least to some degree," suggested Milly with a tone of confidence and a seeming grasp of the situation that overcame Camden's initial reluctance.

"What do you think, Jones?" asked Camden.

"Sounds good, but won't our observers pick up the extra body?" Jones asked quizzically.

"That is a strong possibility..." Camden agreed. "What can we do about it. . . It is a risk we have to take."

"Maybe not," said Milly. "I am about the same size as Smith... Why not take her back out with you and leave me in her place. The body count remains the same and nobody outside is any the wiser. Besides

The Mammoth Incident

she can brief the Superintendent on what has been going on down here far better than we can, based on our limited observations."

"Sounds like the thing to do ... I'll send her over in a few minutes after we make the rounds one more time and get a wish list together. It will give us an opportunity to let people know what is happening," affirmed Jones.

While it seemed like hours, it was actually only about 35 minutes before the female park ranger Smith moved toward the supply cache. Milly hopped down and embraced Smith who was happy to see a familiar face after the hours of confinement. With a push from Milly and the pull of Camden's outstretched arm Smith gained the ledge. A few minor adjustments to Milly's head gear and Smith was ready to go.

Climbing up the chimney took a little more time and effort than coming down, but was manageable enough. Camden and Smith moved through the opening to the top of the breakdown without delay. In a combination of sliding and jumping, they moved down the rock slope sending cascades of rock crashing down with every jump and slide they took. The descent was noisy but quick.

A moment at the bottom to knock off some of the dust and adjust their head gear and the two headed down the corridor. Camden taking the lead since he presumably knew the way.

Camden turned to ask Smith how she was doing. In his concern for another he saved himself. He heard the report of the revolver before he felt the searing pain in the back of his right arm.

Camden started to slowly raise himself off the ground and then stopped and remained prone while he tried to gather his thoughts. He consciously returned his pistol to its holster and as he did so he saw the collapsed form of Smith but a few feet away, gun in hand. Two small holes in her chest trickled blood. Only then did Camden understand what his lightning reflexes had done. He had killed Smith.

Realizing the source of the attack had been effectively eliminated Camden raised to his feet, picked up his helmet and moved to the crumpled form. He placed his hand on her neck looking for a sign of life he did not expect to find. He knew death well and nothing here suggested otherwise. As he started to remove his hand a glitter of a gold chain caught his eye and he slipped his hand under the fine links. A medallion identical to the one he had found earlier slid into his hand. Satisfied it was indeed the same as the one he already held in his possession, he released it to let it slip under Smith's shirt.

Camden wondered how this would go over with Superintendent Hicks for now there was an additional body to remove from the cave. He could not help but think that in two visits, two people had died. One at his hand.

Camden slipped through the vee shaped passage to the main cavern. Walking up the passage he pondered his next move.

The Mammoth Incident

"Halt, who goes there?" came a voice out of nowhere.

Camden was on the pavement with his gun in hand and rolling for cover before he realized what had startled him.

"Easy, easy... don't shoot... don't shoot. You must be Camden. We are the army and we are on your side," affirmed the source of the mystery voice.

Camden breathed again. Sheer terror had clutched his chest until now. He could see the uniform and the M 16 of a young soldier stepping from behind some rock formations off to one side. He had seen the insignia before and recognized it as belonging to the counter terrorist attack group put together by the Department of Defense to deal with air hijackings and other terrorist activities. They had a reputation for being effective.

"You gave me a start... Sorry. Yes, I am Camden," Camden spoke softly but audibly as he holstered his gun and got to his feet. "This cave contains a lot of surprises... Some of which can be lethal."

"Captain Fitzgerald, sir. It is a pleasure to meet you," said the captain extending a hand toward Camden. "Our job is to secure the cave and the grounds for now. We plan to isolate and neutralize the terrorists as soon as the opportunity presents itself."

"Fine, I am certain you will do just that when the time comes. However, there may be a problem in finding that opportunity... ," Camden responded as he shook hands with the Captain. His voice trailing with the second part of his comment.

"What was that?" said the captain.

"Just an observation on the elusiveness of this particular group of terrorists," Camden responded. "Would you radio ahead that I am on my way to Superintendent Hicks?"

"Yes sir, right away," replied the Captain.

Camden turned and walked to the elevators. He passed a number of men crouched behind various objects within the cave. None acknowledged him verbally although all were aware of his presence.

Chapter Eleven

Later That Day

"Stall for time... that is the key... keep talking with them until they lower their guard and then we take them out." The remarks of a FBI authority on terrorism didn't strike a responsive cord with Camden.

Instead unanswerable questions ran through his head. "Talk to whom?" The messages had all been one sided coming from the terrorist with no return address. "Take out whom?" No one, except possibly himself, had even seen a terrorist. "How could one eliminate something that for the moment didn't have any tangible form?" Camden sat quietly in the corner of Superintendent Hicks' office as the dialogue continued. His mood changing as his mind shifted between amusement and bewilderment at some of the points being put forth with such enthusiasm crashed into the brick walls of reality. Strike forces ready to strike with no one to strike. FBI agents ready to arrest with no one to arrest. Paramedics ready to evacuate with no one to take and so it went.

The room was actually crowded. Where before Hicks, McCoy and Camden had sat around the superintendents desk, now a couple of large tables had been brought in with a dozen or so folding chairs. Representatives from the military, the FBI, the President and high Park Service Officials vied for position around the tables. Superintendent Hicks' role in the proceedings was shifting from center stage to that of a support liaison representing the local component of the Park Service. In some sense he had become a "gopher," the office boy sent to run errands and gather data because others had to tend to more "important" things.

Camden saw this happening and wondered if anyone in the room knew the area and the people in it to the degree that Hicks did. A valuable resource was being wasted, but this was the way of bureaucracy and Camden knew this was not the time or the place to change an ingrained component associated with bureaucrats down through the ages.

Camden slipped out of the meeting, if anyone asked, he would indicate he had to go to the bathroom. No one asked or even seemed to see him leave. That he wanted a little mental space was of little, if any, consequence to those present.

"Camden. Here is the information you wanted on that piece of wire," Shirley handed a memo pad to him as he turned to acknowledge his name.

Written on the pad was the name of a local supplier and the names of his three biggest customers in the last year. Hicks had known who to call and had instructed Shirley accordingly. "I didn't know if you wanted me to bring this into the meeting, so I just kept it until I got a chance to talk to you. I hope I have done the right thing."

"You did just fine. I doubt anyone in there has any idea what this might mean... Thanks. In fact don't mention it to anyone except Hicks," Camden answered casting a disdainful look to the office door he had just

The Mammoth Incident

closed. "Have you seen King lately. . . the pilot who flew me in here?"

"Yes, as a matter of fact he left word with me that he would be down with the chopper pilots. They are over in the east parking lot. He said if you asked that was where he could be found," Shirley responded with a smile, pleased that she could contribute in some small way. A feeling she was not getting from the individuals utilizing Hicks' office.

****

"Are you sure this thing is airworthy?" inquired Camden as he eased into the passenger seat of the vintage Cessna 172.

"Trust me," replied a sardonic King as he buckled in. A couple of twists and pulls on the flight controls, one prime to the engine, a twist of the starter switch and the engine came to life with a roar. King began to taxi to the runway doing the preflight checklist as the plane rolled.

Camden didn't know how to take this. He decided the quick ignition of the engine was a good sign and considering his past experience with King at the controls figured he had little to worry about if skill at flying was the key.

King put the throttle to the fire wall and the Cessna began to pick up speed. Before it was really ready to fly King jumped the Cessna into the air relying on a cushion of air known as ground effect to keep it airborne until sufficient speed was picked up to climb out at a standard climb rate.

"Lets take a pass over the park before it gets dark," yelled Camden to King over the engine noise.

King nodded and turned more sharply than Camden's stomach really appreciated, and in minutes the main headquarters building was visible below. A pair of army helicopters sat in the parking lot east of the building.

"Head south along that route," shouted Camden, suggesting the retracing of the route run the previous day by the Chevy he had chased to the lake.

Below spatial relationships took on a different perspective when viewed from the air. The route seen from the air looked much more direct than the winding curves Camden remembered from the chase. A big old yellow school bus sat at the edge of a campground just the other side of a grouping of trees that blocked the view from the administration building. Camden until now had no idea that such a campground existed in such close proximity to the main complex of buildings. A closer look revealed partly why not. The access road actually ran off in a rather obtuse direction and then doubled back on itself. Some clever planner had purposely done this to create a sense of isolation that campers tend to prefer. Only someone paying close attention on the ground or in an airplane would realize the close proximity of the campground to "civilization."

On the horizon a late sun reflected off a body

The Mammoth Incident

of water that Camden took to be the reservoir he had visited the previous day. King set up a course that would take the plane over the part of the lake where Camden had last seen the powerboat.

Although Camden had been prepared by Hick's remarks that the only house in that area was the very one he had visited just a few days earlier on his arrival, he still could not fully comprehend the grandeur of the estate. From the car, on the drive in, only bits and pieces of its rolling grounds had been revealed. The view from the air gave a much truer picture of the palatial scale. It also showed the perimeter of the stone fence topped with barbed wire that surrounded the entire property where it fronted access roads through the area.

"Boy, I would sure like to know what is going on down there," Camden shouted into King's right ear.

"Why don't you drop in and find out?" a smiling King suggested in a curiously sarcastic and yet serious vein.

"What do you mean by that?" inquired Camden.

King motioned over his shoulder to the back of the plane. Camden's eyes followed coming to rest on a couple of parachutes.

"What are those doing here?" asked Camden.

"I wasn't sure if this plane was airworthy so I brought them along just in case," replied a smiling King. "As a matter of fact this plane belongs to the local skydiver group and while I was negotiating the use of the plane I got the use of a couple of chutes thrown in just in case you wanted to work on your night parachuting technique."

"Just what I really wanted to do," Camden smiled as he slid the seat back along the floor tracks to the rear of the plane. He recognized the brand of parachute as one with excellent control characteristics in the hand of an experienced jumper. While he didn't perceive himself as an expert he did know how to get around with one when he had to. One hundred jumps to his credit may have had something to do with his confidence even if he wasn't particularly enthusiastic about the idea of jumping this particular evening.

"Did you see that opening to the west of the mansion house?" asked Camden.

"Got it. Looks like a natural. Winds from the south at five knots. I'll set you up a departure point from which even a blind person could hit the mark," King's smile was a little tighter, and it was obvious he was getting down to the serious subtleties of getting the jumper as well aligned with the drop zone as was possible from the pilot's perspective.

Camden slipped his seat back as far as it would go on the two steel racks that carried it. The parachute looked to be in good shape if a cursory examination of the case would reveal anything. He knew it wouldn't. So once again he would have to trust to luck or something stronger that the case contained what he and King understood to be in it.

The Mammoth Incident

With a few contortions all the necessary straps were secured. Even a helmet was available. Camden wondered how far ahead this man King was thinking.

"Ten seconds to drop... Are you about ready?" King asked.

Camden moved the seat forward a bit, unlatched the door and eased himself onto the wing strut step. He motioned to King with a thumbs-up sign to which King nodded an acknowledgement.

A few seconds later King motioned his hand toward Camden. While not rehearsed, Camden knew the time had come to step off. A quick glance to confirm his bearings and Camden slipped into the darkness. King thought he heard a muffled, "Oh shit..." above the engine noise as Camden dropped from sight. King re-trimmed the aircraft and flew on as if nothing had happened. He didn't even try to see the opened chute below him. It was not a lack of concern for Camden's welfare. On the contrary, he knew the only way he could visually check was to bring the aircraft around abruptly. Such a maneuver would surely attract attention from even an unconcerned observer on the ground. What it would do for someone supposedly standing watch as a security person was a whole another matter that King didn't want to get into.

Camden dropped like a rock for about five seconds and pulled the rip cord. The reassuring jerk to the harness indicated the canopy had deployed properly and he reached for the guides. Glancing upward he was relieved that the canopy was some dark hue and not a white or similarly light color that would have given him away if anyone was looking. Checking his orientation he pulled as necessary to spin the chute around and head it toward the clearing he had previously selected in the aircraft.

It was a textbook jump. Camden hit the ground with his knees slightly bent. As he hit he collapsed and rolled on his right thigh and hip. A slight ground roll and he was up and pulling in the parachute. The pounding of his heart made him realize just how long it had been since his last jump. Could it be possible? Five years since the last daytime jump, maybe seven or eight since the last night jump. In any event this evening jump wasn't into a swamp with the assorted creatures that Camden would just as soon forget about.

Listening for sounds above his heart beat Camden quickly rolled the parachute into a tight ball and thrust it and himself under the boughs of an evergreen on the perimeter of the opening. His ears straining for any man made sound could not miss the distinctive sound of the Great Horned Owl somewhere up on the adjacent ridge. The call was met by another, a bit fainter, perhaps, but still recognizable, from the ridge across the valley. Other assorted sounds drifted through the clearing but none that sounded to be man made or made by man's best friend. Camden was relieved by this and the fact that his heart was beginning to sound less deafening.

The Mammoth Incident

Easing out from under the pine tree he opted to stay close to the edge of the clearing as he proceeded in the direction of the manor house faintly silhouetted up the hill from his location. A band of secondary mixed hardwoods stood between him and the more formal gardens he had visited a few days earlier.

Well into the band of hardwoods Camden was not sure which he sensed first - the musty odor or the muted grunts. In any event as his eyes attempted to focus in the direction of the apparent source, a large dark shadow adjacent to an old gnarled oak transformed into a very solid dark mass which was coming at an unbelievable speed straight for the same opening in the underbrush in which Camden was standing. Camden leaped to one side. His pant leg brushed by one of the two razor sharp protrusions sported by this very solid aberration.

In no more than a heartbeat the freight train like momentum of the creature stopped. The beast turned, lowered its head and pawed the ground snorting. At the same moment a hole in the dark clouds masking the moon passed through a beam of light that fairly glistened off the creature's shining tusks.

For some reason the creature hesitated, perhaps blinded by the intensity of the moonlight. In that instant Camden cheated destiny again. Grabbing a low branch he swung upward and out of reach as the boar cut furrows in the ground where an instant before he had been.

"Hey big fellow, you can have all the truffles you find. I've just developed an aversion to them that you wouldn't believe," Camden spoke quietly to the beast in what he hoped was a soothing voice. "I'm just passing through on my way to the big house and didn't realize I was on your territory. Hope you will forgive the intrusion. I promise not to do it again."

Instinctively Camden reached for his handgun. Just as his rational mind told him to forget it. He couldn't risk the sound of shooting this creature. His reflex action shot back the message that his gun was not to be found in its usual place. The creature who had momentarily stopped his cultivating looked up at Camden. Its rage building, the creature again turned to dissipating it on the environment in immediate proximity to the main trunk of the tree supporting Camden. Camden thought he could make out the faint outlines of his gun in the moss and dirt below. Before he was certain, the beast began rotating the soil and everything else with his powerful snout. A cold shiver went up Camden's spine as he envisioned the weapon discharging under the continuing onslaught of this overgrown shoat. "Hey big fellow, be careful, that thing is loaded," Camden whispered in frustration.

As if in contempt the boar threw its nose in the air and in so doing tossed the gun, which it had just snagged on its tusk, a full foot into the air. Camden gasped anticipating the worst. The gun hit an exposed root with a hollow thud but did not discharge.

The Mammoth Incident

Beads of sweat formed profusely on Camden's forehead and merged one with another until tiny rivulets formed and ran down his cheeks to join others coming from other water sheds experiencing similar flooding conditions.

The boar seemed to take on human attributes, at least from Camden's perspective. It circled the base of the tree and looked at Camden with an air of distaste and disdain. With a final grunt the beast slowly ambled off into the night exuding an air of contempt and disdain that nearly masked the pungent musty odor that Camden would never forget as long as he lived. Later in future telling of this tale the wild Russian boar would take on attributes of a reincarnated demon complete with fire red eyes and equally hot breath.

Camden eased through the forest stopping several times thinking he smelt the musty odor of wild boar. Each time he concluded that it was either his over stimulated imagination or that if an odor was present at least the most tangible part one had to worry about was not.

Easing through the forest underbrush was now pretty easy, if one excluded the occasional pangs of apprehension brought on by the actual or perceived odor of wild boar. Camden was actually following what appeared to be a beaten path through the forest that was heading in the general direction that he wanted to go. It was not a formal path in any manicured traditional sense. More like a path made by the passage of animals over the years. Just what species of animals had carved this path Camden could only speculate. His speculations included the friends of, or perhaps the very boar with whom he had earlier become acquainted. In any event he was prepared to yield to the rightful owner if such owner were to present oneself.

Ahead a large limb jutted out over the pathway at a height of little concern to most creatures including boars. However, for a man to avoid it would involve crawling under or stepping off to one side to circumvent the obstruction. Camden chose the later, not wanting to meet friend boar on his own terms, with his four appendages to the ground rather than two.

As Camden touched the protruding branch to ease by, it fell abruptly knocking him off balance. It crashed to the ground missing his right foot by centimeters. Out of the corner of his eye Camden caught a glimpse of a small noose whipping into the air. From his vantage point on the ground he deduced that others were out to get friend boar.

Climbing from the ground and brushing himself off, Camden muttered, "These people just don't have any appreciation for Russian culture of any kind."

Traveling the rest of the distance to the formal gardens was uneventful if one could exclude the tension created by thinking about lurking Russian boars and deadfalls set out to get them. It took a lot

The Mammoth Incident

to unnerve Camden, but it would not be unfair to say the threshold of that point was getting closer than he wanted to admit.

Darting from one clump of roses to another Camden made his way to the courtyard of the manor house. He moved when the moon was masked behind the scattered clouds and visibility seemed at a minimum. Once he misjudged the location of a plant and found himself painfully extricating his left arm from a bush he had not intended to touch much less embrace. A marker at the base of the plant indicated a variety known as "Gentle American Beauty." Camden decided he would not go out of his way to incorporate that variety in any future dealings with the plant world.

Only a few rooms in the house appeared to be lit. Based on his earlier tour it seemed the servants quarter, the master bedroom, and a secondary bedroom or two were about all that were brightly lit. The main entrance and the adjoining foyer area were partially lit but not to the degree that anyone was probably active in these areas.

Camden had decided on the ride down that the room he wanted to check out, if at all possible, was the combination study and recording studio pointed out in passing on his previous tour. The room was situated on the second floor of the building and looked out over the formal garden. A small wrought iron porch, more for looks than use, was situated such that the bay windows could be opened outward to give a relatively unobstructed view of the garden.

The room was dimly lit leading Camden to believe it was not in use. A rather thick and well established coating of ivy covered much of the manor house and this face was no exception. In fact a rather vigorous plant grew up along the very porch that Camden wanted to reach. Things seemed quiet enough and Camden decided it was superfluous to waste further time. He moved below the porch and eased himself onto the ivy securing foot holds and hand holds as he went. The vine was everything he hoped it would be, strong and resilient from years of optimum growing conditions. Another foot up and he could reach the wrought iron of the porch with little difficulty.

Groping above for the next hand hold he circled his hand around a good inch thick portion of vine and began to shift his weight. With the vine taking the bulk of the load he proceeded to release the grip of his other hand to go for the ironwork. As he did so he felt the inch vine give way. A first it was barely perceptible and he was not sure it was happening. In another moment there was no doubt. As he tried to regain his hand hold with the free hand a slab of stucco material bounced off his right shoulder and then bounced away from the building to shatter noisily on the tile patio below.

Tears welled in his eyes as he endured the sharp pangs of pain that nearly overwhelmed him. His free hand now grasping vine and wall almost through

The Mammoth Incident

sheer will power rather than any reasonable purchase in his grip. Above a light went on and the window of the study opened.

"There it is... another bit of that stucco from the chimney breaking loose again. I thought you were going to get that fixed?" A female voice inquired in a manner of condemnation that only a female tone can properly deliver.

"The masons are coming next week. Given the current state of affairs it hardly seemed advisable to have additional strangers milling around," responded the male voice.

Chuckling, "You do have a point there, I won't fault you for that... I think I will go read for a while and go to bed. It sounds like things are pretty well under control on our end. I never thought they would be so passive given the stakes involved," retorted the female voice changing from a rather warm response to a much more calculated and detached tone.

"Don't underestimate them my dear... Oh yes, the workings of the bureaucrats are slow and predictable. It is those dedicated public service types that one has to be fearful of," concluded the male voice drawing the window shut while he talked.

Camden decided he could start to breath again anytime his body wanted to start functioning again. As it did so, he became aware of the pain in his shoulder which seemed to intensify the harder he held on with his right hand. His grip with the left hand never was really a grip and had just stopped faking it. The result was that his body was twisting away from the wall and the vine in a manner that would wrench him loose any second. With a concerted effort Camden put every ounce of energy into a convulsive snap that brought him within striking range of the wrought iron porch. A last desperate thrust of his left arm brought him the grip on the bottom most rail that meant the difference between continuing his imitation of Spiderman and doing an equally good imitation of Humpty Dumpty.

While Camden hung motionless in a suspended state between vine and porch, the lights in the room went off and he could hear a door close. Presumably both individuals had left the room. Releasing his death-like hold on the vine Camden pulled himself up and on to the porch. No small feat given the throbbing ache of a badly bruised and sprained shoulder. The good news was that it was not broken. Pressed against the edge of the porch and the side edge of the window he decided to go for broke. If they were still in there he was going to have to do a lot of explaining. If they were gone, as he believed, he could scope things out at his leisure. Using his penknife he lifted the latch on the windows, eased them open enough to squeeze through and entered the room. The room was empty as he anticipated and his heart rate began to slow, seemingly reacting to the facts of the situation and not Camden's speculations.

Moonlight flooded into the room when the scattered cloud cover permitted. The blue and red light of a variety of digital clocks about the room

The Mammoth Incident

revealed a den lined with built in book cases, most filled with books. A desk on one wall contained the cathode ray screen of a personal computer and the keyboard to operate it. A pair of disk drives were to the right of the monitor. On the shelves behind were a variety of recording and transmitting devices including such things as CB scanners and other devices that looked a bit more powerful. A copy machine and a shredder were on wheeled carts in another corner of the room adjacent to a walk-in safe. Nearby rows of filing cabinets had been set in where a few shelves had been removed. The quality of the work was such that one would hardly notice the difference if one could forget that fire proof steel filing cabinets were not in vogue during the time frame in which the mansion was constructed.

Camden glanced around the room and wondered what it was he hoped to find here anyway. The conversation heard at the window seemed to fit, but then did it? Nothing was actually said that really linked the activity at the cave with the people here. Yet the pair in the boat, where were they going if not here? While Camden pondered these thoughts his eye came to rest on the CB unit. At first he couldn't figure what was unusual about it. Sure, some people monitor channel 9. But then it hit him. The receiver was connected by a wire cable to a small black box which sat on the edge of the desk with the PC. It, in turn, was connected to the PC and the wire used was the same as that he had picked up in the cave. As he bent over to examine the unknown device in greater detail he heard a door latch shut and foot falls down the hall. In an instant he moved past a free standing combination bulletin and chalk board. Nearly knocking it over in his haste, he just barely steadied it and eased through the window when the door to the studio opened. Camden heard this from his hastily acquired position on the porch. He was pressed tightly up against the edge of the window and the rail. The lights came on in the room and Camden watched breathlessly as the shadow on the window curtain indicated the figure causing it was moving to the window. The windows were pushed open to arms length. He heard a breath drawn in, held and then released. The windows were drawn shut and the sound of their latching was just barely perceptible above the din of Camden's heart.

    Feeling like Spiderman again Camden thought that while he couldn't stay here forever it might not hurt to stick around for a few more minutes. At first he couldn't figure out what he was hearing. He recognized the printer cranking away. It was a dot matrix with its characteristic whine as it spewed forth. Other sounds seemed to be the chirps and clucks of disk drives working. It was that initial audio squawk that puzzled him the most. He had almost forgotten about it when he heard it again. This time he heard some keyboard action coupled with the whirring and clicking of the disk drives. A few minutes later the shredder whirred for a second or more and it was

The Mammoth Incident

over. Who ever was in the room turned out the lights and left. Camden felt pretty ridiculous hanging to the side of the building and eased down the vine to the ground only a shade less faster and gentler than if he had fallen.

Chapter Twelve

Well away from the house and under cover of a large evergreen Camden pondered his next move. He couldn't recall making any plans with King to airlift him out of this place, and as a matter of fact he could not recall any conversations with King or anybody else about what was supposed to happen next. The obvious solution was to hoof-it down to the road and then either walk or hitchhike back. Camden wondered who would pick up a hitchhiker at such an hour particularly in the disheveled condition that he was in. The walking alternative didn't sound that great either since it could easily be twenty miles back to base if one knew the way and he only had a general sense of the direction, let alone a road map.

Camden noticed what appeared to be an old carriage building not too far away. The double modern garage doors suggested that old carriages had long since given way to the horseless variety and if a car was to be found this was the logical place to look first.

A side door to the structure was not locked and Camden eased in. Everything seemed quiet. A fluorescent above a workbench provided illumination, apparently twenty four hours a day. Camden was surprised to find not one car but four. Furthermore, instead of the matched set of Cadillacs or Mercedes he had expected, the collection consisted of vehicles all at least 25 years old.

On further examination he found that the car in the front, closest to the door was the very one he

The Mammoth Incident

had seen outrun the sheriff's car the night he had arrived. Small world, thought Camden. He moved up to the car and glanced inside through the open window on the driver's side. The key was in the ignition and it looked like it was ready to run. Camden reflected for a moment and decided beggars, let alone car thieves, can't be choosy. All that remained was to open the garage door and to get the hell out of there. Camden moved to try the door and found that it was tied into an electric door opener and could not be opened at the door but needed to be activated from a switch or some other remote control device. He returned and looked into the vintage machine and attached to the dash appeared to be the very device he was seeking, the button to activate the door. He eased himself onto the front seat of the car and pulled the door shut.

"Hey, what are you doing in here?" came an abrupt challenging shout. A large muscular man moved toward the car from the rear of the building.

Camden's heart leaped. He was not expecting to be discovered at this moment and was taken completely by surprise. In the instant it took to regain his composure he hit the garage door button and turned the ignition key. The Hudson fired off instantly, allowing Camden to breath a sigh of relief.

The man had closed to within a few feet of the car and Camden could see him coming out of the corner of his eye. The time it took for him to close the distance was all that was needed for the garage door to lift sufficiently that the car could clear. Camden smiled at the sneering face peering into the open window as he floored the accelerator and popped the clutch. In a squeal of burning rubber the Hudson moved from the garage and down the drive accelerating with every foot of motion.

"Wow, I don't remember these buggies having this sort of acceleration," Camden said to himself as the car roared down the drive. The steel gate to the estate loomed ahead in the headlights as Camden braked hard to de-accelerate the vehicle and avoid crashing into what looked to be a rather formidable barrier. Hoping against hope he hit the button on the dash that had activated the overhead door. It worked, the gate started to move, slowly but nevertheless opening. Camden waited patiently for what seemed like an eternity as the giant gate slid to one side. As the opening approached a size that the car could fit through, a flash of light in the rear view mirror signaled the approach of a vehicle from behind. Camden looked over his shoulder in disbelief at the vintage Ford bearing down on him. Popping the clutch the Hudson shot through the opening and careened onto the highway. Moments later the Ford cleared the gate and similarly careened onto the highway.

"Why does it always seem like the car I'm chasing is getting away and yet when I am being chased it always seems like they are gaining on me in spite of myself?" Camden mused aloud to himself. The Ford was clearly gaining and Camden knew why. He

The Mammoth Incident

didn't know the neighborhood, much less the road and he continually strained to see beyond the headlights in an effort to anticipate the curves or other obstacles ahead as he careened into the darkness at speeds approaching a hundred miles per hour. The driver of the Ford was obviously in familiar territory for he knew when to speed up for straightaways and when to cut to the inside for curves and in so doing was reducing the distance between the two cars rapidly.

Camden pondered the situation considering the options. He could always shoot the would be assailant if it got too tight. Why not, he had done it before! Somehow Camden felt that shooting was not called for in this situation and just really wanted to get this turkey off his back. Introducing gunfire would only escalate the gravity of the encounter to a point that Camden did not want if it could be avoided.

In the deep recesses of his mind Camden recalled an old Robert Mitchum movie he had seen as a kid. The title was *Thunder Road* and it was about moonshiners running whiskey through the mountains. Perhaps the very ones he was now traversing. In the film Mitchum's character is battling it out with someone who is trying to run him off the read. Mitchum prevails by tossing a lighted cigarette into the lap of his opponent and in the resulting distraction forces him off the road into a power transformer. The idea had merit but Camden wondered how to proceed given that he didn't smoke.

Camden's thought processes jarred as the

Hudson reverberated from the impact of the Ford into the rear bumper. The pursuer had closed the distance while Camden's mind had wandered. Undaunted, Camden was terrified.

Spying a cigarette lighter protruding from the dash of the car, Camden decided, "Why not? It worked for Mitchum it ought to work for me," he said pushing the lighter button in. He observed the Ford moving up on his left side. One additional small problem, the window on the passenger side of the Ford was fully closed. Camden gestured to the driver of the Ford he wanted to talk and motioned to crank down the window. For some unknown reason the driver leaned over and did just that. Before words were exchanged Camden grabbed the cigarette lighter and hurled it into the lap of the Ford's driver. At the same instance he swerved the Hudson sharply into the side of the Ford.

The Ford started to fishtail as the driver fought to regain control. "Wow," yelled Camden, "just like in the movies!" In the same instance the Hudson rebounding from the impact rolled a right tire off the side of the asphalt and clipped against the guardrail. As Camden pulled to bring the car back onto the roadway, the road veered sharply to the left. A new set of guardrails appeared directly ahead as the Hudson lurched left and went into a slide. Camden could see nothing but blackness in the rear view mirror as the car slid backward through the guardrail and down the ravine bowing saplings and bouncing off

The Mammoth Incident

more substantial trees and rocks as it went. Camden caught one last glimpse of the Ford still fishtailing, seemingly out of control, but nevertheless oscillating from one side to the other of the centerline in the highway. The driver may have had some problems but was still keeping the car on the road and that was more than Camden could say about himself.

The sickening sounds of metal scraping against rock and trees finally subsided. Camden looked out into the forest through the opening in the side of the car where the door had been. In the slide it had been peeled back like a banana skin and was now pressed against the front fender. In his lap was a pile of glass particles that had been the rear window. Smashed to smithereens by a tree branch that entered from the rear and actually protruded out the front just to the right of where Camden's head had been. Pulling himself out of the impression he had made in the seat he gingerly stepped from the car only to collapse into a heap as his footing slipped out from under on a moss covered rock.

Camden slowly lifted himself up off the ground. He chose his footing more carefully and brushed glass and bits of humus off his pants. The smell of gasoline was quite apparent and this encouraged him to scramble up the hillside even before he noticed a set of lights coming from the direction he had just traveled. Nearing the crest of the ravine a muffled blast of igniting gasoline and the resulting push of hot air returned him to the ground.

George R. Harker

From his vantage point he watched the lights loom and a vehicle take form in the darkness. It was a pickup truck with an insignia on the side much like the Park Service vehicle he had ridden in the other day.

He heard the door slam as the driver got out and walked to the edge of the road for a better look at the burning Hudson. It was ace pilot King.

"What are you doing here?" asked Camden from the ground.

A startled King, "Looking for you, I couldn't quite imagine you walking back, but I must admit I wasn't prepared for the old Hudson and the Ford routine. You sure have a knack for getting into some strange situations." King smiled as he offered Camden a hand and pulled him from the ground. "By the way where is the Ford?"

"Last I saw it, it was fish tailing down the highway in that direction," Camden motioned in the direction he had last seen the car as he spoke. "It was supposed to be down there not me. Let us get out of here before he comes back, if he comes back. Do you know another way back to the park?"

"Actually, we have to go the other direction to get to the park. If you go this way far enough and long enough you will end up in Louisville," laughed King.

"I never did have much sense of direction."

Chapter Thirteen

Milly moved about from one group of people to another tending more to psychological needs than physical injuries, although there were a few bruises and even some broken bones that required some attention. As luck would have it there had been a physician in the group when the cave-ins occurred and he had given the appropriate first-aid. People were referring to the unlikely chain of events as a cave-in. Perhaps it was easier to accept the predicament they were in if it could be attributed to acts of nature rather than the acts of their fellow man even when one knew the truth, as all did.

The tour group had broken into smaller subunits. Some of the units were composed of members of a family on vacation. Other groups where composed of couples drawn together by their similar status in life. Still another group was composed of the remaining members who didn't seem to fit into any other particular group.

Each group seemed to have gravitated to it's own special place in the cave. Some moved into shallow pockets in the perimeters while others clustered in the open, sitting on boulders rolled into a circle. Some sat on civil defense blankets placed on the ground much as one would do on a Sunday picnic or on a trip to the beach. The activity at each of the clusters ran the gamut from pure boredom to genuine bouts of pure creativity as some played trivia games making up the rules as they went along.

It was against this background that Milly

circulated, moving from one group to another. Her presence as a ranger different than the one that had been there initially was only noticed by a few. Most just saw a female park service ranger and didn't realize a switch had been made. The few that had noticed the difference and said something were taken into partial confidence and told that efforts were underway to free the group and to stay calm. Most accepted this, if not fully understanding how this was to come about.

"Ladies and gentlemen, may I have your attention please," the amplified voice echoed through the cave and indeed attracted everyone's attention in an instant. "As you may know, your safe exit from this place is contingent on the payment of a large sum of money to a repository of our choosing. As of this moment that payment has not been made and appropriate actions must be taken to assure the authorities that they have no other choice but to comply with our request or suffer grave consequences. Regrettably those grave consequences involve all of you. If our demands are not met in the near future one of you will die in the next twelve hours."

A silent tension permeated the cave. No one moved, stunned by the revelation of the unseen voice and by the very voice itself. The stillness gave way to darkness as the cave lights ceased to function for some seemingly unknown reason. Only later would the connection between the voice and the lights be realized.

The Mammoth Incident

Calm gave way to panic. Screams of terror and anguish bounced off the stone walls.

"Turn on the flashlight," someone yelled.

A cigarette lighter flashed and a spot of flame illuminated a face in a cluster of people at one side of the cave. Then another flicker as a candle was lit. Then another and another came to life. Until the cave was illuminated by spots of light scattered about. The screams and cries diminished in direct proportion to the number of flickering candle lights present.

Milly eased to her feet from the crouched position next to a large rock which many thousands of years ago had been part of the cave's roof. As she stepped off to join with a group fifty feet from her, a hand reached around her waist from behind and to her right. Given the tension in the air she grabbed the hand and the attached arm plus person and in a continuous movement of her body hurled the attacker against the ground. A rather shaken 250 pounds of truck driver lay prone on his back and stared blankly in the direction of the ceiling. Milly bent over to examine her handiwork as others in close enough proximity to know what had happened moved over for a closer look.

"What was that all about?" asked an onlooker.

"I'm not really sure," responded Milly. "I felt this arm around my waist and I thought someone was attacking me."

A bottle of smelling salts was whiffed by the nose of the unconscious form. Slowly it took effect and a noticeable shudder rippled through the prostrate form. "Where am I?" asked a faint confused voice sounding quite small, considering the size of the body from which it emanated.

"You are trapped in Mammoth Cave just like the rest of us," replied the physician administering the smelling salts, "Why did you attack the ranger?"

"What ranger? What attack? Oh... now I remember... I... Oh God, no... I wasn't attacking anyone... I was just... just...scared. I just needed to hold someone," the man spoke almost incoherently and started to sob convulsively.

"It is all right," said Milly. "Now I understand. I just didn't realize what was happening."

Milly breathed deeply as she tried to calm herself. She truly understood or thought she did, but that still didn't stop the adrenalin coursing through her veins. She moved back to sit against the rock where she had been sitting before. She had intended to close her eye momentarily to blot out the images surrounding her in the cave. More exhausted than she had realized, it would be another five hours until she would open them again.

When she opened them again it was as if nothing had happened for the lights were again on in the cave. A hush fell over the group as each wondered why the lights had chosen this particular time to come on, as if the lights had a mind of their own and would go on or off at their own whim.

The hushed silence was short lived. People

The Mammoth Incident

began to talk in subdued whispers that eased up to normal conversational tones. Order appeared to be returning to the group as people returned to the small subgroups which they had inhabited earlier.

A sharp scream coursed through the cave and echoed off the walls and ceilings shattering the conversational tones as well as the conversations themselves in the same single instant. All heads turned toward a sheltered cove of the cave that by mutual agreement was the male latrine.

About twenty feet in front and to one side of the opening lay the prostrate body of a man. The handle of a hunting knife protruded upward from the middle of his back. The woman standing over the form and screaming uncontrollably was his wife.

Milly and the physician ran to the hysterical woman. Milly to give comfort to the lady, the physician to confirm what everyone who could see the knife handle already knew. Death had been quick and quiet. The killer was obviously knowledgeable about human anatomy and just where to place the lethal blade with minimum effort.

Chapter Fourteen

Camden felt better for the rest. Five hours of sleep may not have been as good as eight but given the level of abuse that his body had been subjected to in the last twenty four hours it seemed considerably more than adequate. Although he had a great deal on his mind the last five hours had seemed like five minutes. His conscious mind had totally shut down from exhaustion and he had slept a deep restful sleep oblivious to all externalities.

Among the externalities he missed were the movement of uniformed men carrying rifles with special laser telescopic sights to positions above and below ground in the entire cave complex. Every known entrance had at least two specially equipped sharpshooters stationed in such a manner as to have a clear field of fire if the need arose. The men had been brought in by helicopter. More mundane means of transportation were out of the question for a strike force of this caliber. They were prepared to strike swiftly and effectively once they were given the go ahead and pointed in the general direction of the terrorist. The only difficulty in this situation was that no one seemed to know in what direction to point them.

Camden grabbed a plate of food and a cup of coffee at the commissary tent set up by the army to feed the troops and support personnel which were starting to evolve into a fairly sizeable contingent. With a second cup of coffee in hand he headed over to Hicks' office to see what was going on. Wearing the

The Mammoth Incident

identification badge someone had thoughtfully placed in his room Camden was able to move past sentries that seemed to be stationed at just about every doorway.

The general commotion and the rapid coming and going of personnel from Hicks' inner office suggested to Camden that something significant had happened or was about to happen. When Shirley caught the quizzical glance from Camden she pulled him aside and brought him up to date. There had been a death in the cave... Renewed demand for payment of ransom or else... Camden absorbed the information like a sponge. Interrupting the flow of information occasionally seeking to identify those elements that may have greater significance than initially perceived.

Shirley's briefing complete, Camden slipped into Hicks' office and took a seat against the wall. There he half listened to the bantering back and forth of various "specialists" representing just about every law enforcement or military agency in the United States government while he contemplated the information just received versus his own experiences in the last twelve hours. Somewhere he knew there was a link, a relationship between the events in the cave and the events at the mansion. All he had to do was determine what that relationship was.

Involved with his own thoughts, Camden just about missed it. The bureaucrats, panicked by the killing, had decided to send in a portion of the swat team. The team was to go in via the route used by Camden and Milly. Once in they were to secure the cave, whatever that meant, and remove the hostages by retracing their steps back out of the cave.

Camden started to comment on the inherent difficulties of the plan such as the problem of getting untrained individuals up the small chimney passage. The words were barely out of his mouth when it became apparent to him that very few were listening, much less comprehending the points he was trying to make. Camden cut short his comments and sat down. There would be an assault on the cave by a special team within the hour and no amount of reasoned discussion that spoke against such a plan was to be of any consequence.

Within minutes Camden decided to leave Hicks' office. The single minded determination of the group to pursue what Camden considered a reckless and foolish endeavor was not conducive to the thinking that he was trying to do. His departure from the meeting went virtually unnoticed. Everyone else was caught up in the excitement of doing something. Whether that "something" was the thing to be doing or not was no longer a consideration.

Camden headed out of the building and over to the parking lot that the choppers were using for a landing site. He was hoping to run into King with the idea of exchanging observations and ideas, sort of a mini brainstorming session to see if between the two of them some order or relationship in the events of

The Mammoth Incident

the last 24 hours could be determined.

As he walked slowly in the general direction of the helicopters a squad of men jogged by in a tight formation. Apparently the team chosen to go into the cave. Camden wished them a silent "good luck." His thoughts returning briefly to his two ventures into the cave and the two deaths with which they were associated. Just about to the choppers Camden noticed a jeep virtually sprouting antennas of all types and configurations. Obviously a mobile communications vehicle used to link the ground efforts with the aerial support provided by the choppers. One antenna configuration caught Camden's attention. A dish shaped affair that was moving slowly back and forth as a technician adjusted some dials on the console in front of him. Something in Camden's subconscious triggered on this particular configuration. He knew he had seen something quite similar in the recent past, but he could not get a handle on it just yet. He tried to systematically review the chain of events in the last few days, exploring every tangential thought, hoping to stimulate the recall of the connection, if there was one, to be recalled. After all there had been times in the past when he thought he recognized someone or something and it turned out not to be the case.

Camden was so engrossed in his own mental gymnastics that he was virtually oblivious to his surroundings. So much so that he was totally startled when an unseen force grabbed his arm and yanked him backward and away from the slowly rotating blades of a chopper idling on the pad.

"Easy there, partner. You trying to get your head taken off?" inquired a concerned King. "A few more steps and you would have gotten the haircut of your life."

"What... What are you talking about?" Camden recognized the voice and King but had not put the total situation together. Actually he was trembling from the start given him by King. In another instant, however, Camden realized what had happened or was about to happen and King's role in preventing disaster. "Thanks, I was thinking about the events of the last 24 hours and not really with the present. There is something about that antenna on that jeep but I just can not place it," explained Camden motioning toward the slowly oscillating antenna on the communications jeep.

"Oh, yeah... The one on that jeep? It looks very similar to the one on the mansion the other night," responded King as a matter of fact.

"What? Are you sure?" Camden could hardly contain his excitement and disbelief.

"Sure I am sure, didn't you see that sticking up by the Northeast chimney?" affirmed King confidently.

Camden reflected on that a moment and a series of mental images flashed through his mind; a wild boar, a rose bush, the glint of the moon light on the mansion and others. "Yes, now that you mention it I did recall seeing that antenna when the moon light

The Mammoth Incident

struck the mansion. Perhaps not consciously but yet you are right I can recall it now."

"It is a somewhat unusual piece of equipment for even a real radio buff. The antenna is highly directional and must be tuned carefully to the particular station one is wanting to receive. Such specific tuning cuts down on interference and gives a better signal. However, most ham operators want something that picks up more stations rather than less."

"Would that antenna be focused on the site of the last transmission?" asked Camden.

"It is a possibility. Do you want to check it out?" asked King.

"Can you get us a chopper?"

"Take your pick. These guy's are going crazy sitting around with nothing to do."

"You decide. I'll be right back. I have to get a map." Camden ran into the superintendents office and asked Shirley for a map. The ever efficient Shirley produced the one he was looking for in a matter of seconds.

As the engine whine increased the machine shuddered slightly and moved forward and upward into the air. In seconds the parking lot was well below and Camden could see the teams of men moving about in some sort of seemingly ordered chaos. The pilot had been briefed by King, and the chopper swept toward the reservoir in much the same flight path as they had flown the previous evening. The chopper stayed to one side of the property not wanting to go directly overhead to avoid drawing attention.

The antenna was clearly visible strapped to the stucco sheathed chimney. Camden drew a line on his map depicting the axis of the antenna. Then he drew a second line perpendicular to the first from the approximate center of the antenna as it would appear if placed on the map. The line projected back almost on the very course they had taken to get there. Camden pointed this out to King who just nodded acknowledgement.

"Lets check this out," said Camden over the intercom as he moved forward to the pilot. The pilot took the map and rotated the machine around to pick up a course corresponding to the line Camden had drawn on the map. He also slowed the speed of the craft and dropped to a lower altitude.

Trees, rocks, ridge tops and hollows jumped up and then back as the chopper moved along maintaining a constant altitude. A rather ramshackle cabin flashed into view and Camden asked the pilot to swing around for another and lower look. The pass was made but all indications were that the building had long since been abandoned and not used in any way in recent times. Nevertheless, the location was marked on the map for a ground reconnaissance at a latter time.

Further on the marked course a faint wisp of smoke could be observed drifting up the far end of a hollow. Camden again asked the pilot to make a

The Mammoth Incident

closer and lower pass. Camden leaned out one side of the chopper while King leaned from the other to get a better view of whatever was going on below. The rotor down draft was tossing the branches on the trees and shrubs around. Below Camden could make out the approximate source of the fire. It seemed to be coming from under a pile of junk in proximity to a small collection of various drums and barrels. A lean-to appeared to be built against the face of the rock outcropping that formed one side of the hollow.

"Pull-up! pull-up!" a calm but insistent King spoke forcibly into the intercom with a sense of urgency that the pilot would not ignore. The craft lurched hard as full power was applied and the machine seemed to leap skyward. Camden tightened his grip to keep from falling out, not trusting the restraining harness that secured him to the chopper. At the same instant he too saw the form moving from under a rock outcropping, then the twin muzzle flashes of a double barreled shotgun. In another few seconds he heard the report of the weapon. Closely followed by the patter of spent shot pellets hitting against the aluminum underside of the chopper.

Out of range and out of sight of the ground shooter Camden marked the location on the map as "active still" and asked the pilot to pick up the course again while giving the site a sufficient distance to avoid drawing further fire. The pilot had no difficulty in responding to such a sane and rational request. He had feared the guys in the back might want to go back for a closer look. With that in mind he had been looking for a place to set down if the situation required, such as taking damage from a hit. The difficulty was that nothing visible looked like a suitable place to land, much less crash land.

Camden was surprised when the chopper passed over a line of trees to reveal the campsite in close proximity to the Park Service headquarter buildings and visitor center. While he had been expecting them based on the course drawn on the map he was caught off guard, partly from the incident at the still and partly from the uniformity and monotony of the terrain from that point on. He had lost track of the relative progress over the ground from the lack of significant landmarks. The chopper was coming in over the end of the campground farthest from the administration buildings. In fact a few hundred feet further and the site would have been missed entirely.

The old school bus that he had seen earlier sat at the opposite end of the campground. Given his familiarity with it Camden hardly gave it a second glance as he looked beyond the administration building in the direction the chopper would head as it proceeded along the course dictated by the line on the map. A tap on the shoulder and the outstretched arm of King drew his attention sharply back to the bus. It took his eyes a moment or two to focus on the bus and then he saw it. A small antenna, not unlike the one on the communications jeep, protruding just

The Mammoth Incident

above the middle of the bus. Only a few inches clear of the sheet metal roof and painted the same color as the bus it was a very unobtrusive object. A person on the ground in any proximity to the bus would not have been able to see it.

Camden would have missed it entirely if King had not caught it. It was on King's instructions to the pilot to sweep toward the administration building away from the plotted course that brought the antenna into Camden's clear view. Camden turned to King and nodded. The unspoken exchange reflected their shared belief that they had found what they were seeking and that further air time was unnecessary. King instructed the pilot to land where they had taken off in the parking lot behind the administration building.

The chopper eased over the administration building as the pilot made his approach. Below Camden could see the other choppers were no longer sitting passively on the asphalt, but had their rotors turning as men bearing stretchers moved to load obviously injured soldiers aboard. Before his own craft had completed touchdown, one chopper rotated to face east and then whisked away. In a few more minutes the second chopper followed the first and disappeared. A strange silence hung in the air as the rotor noise dissipated and the choppers faded from view beyond the trees.

"What happened?" Camden asked a young dishevelled, but apparently unhurt, soldier who had just assisted in the loading.

"We were moving up a large rock pile when a voice out of nowhere told us to 'leave or die.' The lieutenant told us to get ready to give covering fire and then to proceed. We had not moved ten feet when some massive boulders at the top started rolling down," the young soldier pausing briefly to try and maintain his composure. "It was like a bowling ball smashing through ten pins and we were the pins."

"I understand," said Camden taking the fellow by the arm and leading him to a group of other soldiers sitting under the shade of a large tree adjacent to the parking lot. "You have done all you can. Sit down and take it easy." Camden motioned for a medic and suggested to him that the lad was suffering from shock. The medic concurred and stayed with the youth while Camden and King moved toward the administration building.

Chapter Fifteen

"All right, all right already. I agree with you there is some connection between the mansion and the school bus, but what has that got to do with the activity in the cave?" asked King.

"I don't know but there must be something," said Camden. "Perhaps Hicks will have some ideas. He doesn't seem to be doing much since the special forces insisted in taking over."

Hicks joined Camden and King in a small supply storage area that Camden and King had been ducking into since Hicks' office was taken over by the special forces.

"The school bus does belong to the Major. We have been letting him park it in that particular spot for years. It is sort of a permanent fixture in the campground. Years back he used to take it out and travel around the country a lot with it. Lately he just keeps it parked there and lets friends of the family use it for weekends or weeks. Not exactly consistent with Park Service policy, but no one has complained and he pays the daily campground rate whether someone is there or not. Matter of fact, had just about forgot about it. It has become such a fixture I hadn't given it any thought until you brought it up," Hicks reported. "Just who is using it now is hard to say. You really think there is some connection between it and what is happening in the cave?"

"I'm sure of it, but don't know how just yet. Does this map mean anything to you?" asked Camden.

"Of course, it is our standard gate map. It

shows the location of our facilities on one side superimposed on some selected underground features half toned in the background," Hicks noted. "On the back is a more detailed rendering of the underground component of the cave system."

"What is the relationship of this particular spot and the surface?" Camden asked Hicks pointing to an 'x' drawn on the map.

"Let me think... That would pretty much correspond to the campground just east of the administration buildings," Hicks indicated.

"The very campground with the school bus parked in it?" Camden noted.

"By golly that is absolutely correct," Hicks acknowledged in astonishment. "In fact it would appear that the 'x' you have there even corresponds to that particular end of the campground where the school bus is located."

King looked at the map over Hick's shoulder and than glanced at Camden. "You think this could be where they are operating the equipment from in the cave? According to this map they would be virtually over the very passage where the people are entrapped."

"An idea worth considering. Punch a hole through the cave ceiling and run some cable down and bingo. It is practically the shortest distance between two points. In addition they are right under out noses and everyone is looking for a much more remote and secluded location. No one ever thought to check right

The Mammoth Incident

here. The idea is truly brilliant, if you think about it," Camden said dryly. "But how are they coordinating with the mansion? There is no hard wire back to it and the radio transmissions are not voice? At least as far as we know."

"You indicated you heard something that sounded like a computer printer when you were outside the window at about the same time the last incident in the cave occurred. Do you think the computer could be the connection?" King asked.

"How would I know? All I know about computers you could write on one small index card. All I recall is that the insignia on the side looked like a multicolored apple. In fact, that must have been what it was, an Apple Computer. It looked just like the ones advertised on TV all the time for the kids. What I wouldn't give for a computer whiz kid right now," Camden asserted in a manner that indicated he was most serious and that he would indeed give just about anything.

"May be able to help you out, Mick. I will be back in a few moments." Hicks indicated as he got up and walked out of the room. Camden and King exchanged glances of perplexity and returned to contemplating the map in front of them.

Twenty minutes later Hicks popped back into the room accompanied by a gangling young man of about 15 or 16, as near as Camden could tell.

"Mick Camden and Jim King this is my son Geoffrey. Geoff is an expert on computers according to his teachers and given my knowledge or perhaps lack of knowledge who am I to argue with their judgement? Perhaps he can help you," Hicks completed the introductions with a smile of fatherly pride brimming from ear to ear.

Camden recounted the computer as he remembered it and the report of static on Channel 9 and the antennas.

"It sounds like they have a modem hooked to the Apple and are transmitting at 1200 baud rate over the voice mode of Channel 9," Geoff indicated in a very nonchalant manner. Seemingly disappointed that the computer question put to him was not more sophisticated.

"What was that? Could you give that to me in plain English that even this computer neophyte could understand?" Camden said meekly with the concurrence of King and Hicks implicit in their looks.

"Well, I will try, sir. Basically they just type in what they want to say into the computer and a little black box next to it translates the written information into a noise signal that is transmitted over the CB. Someone with a receiver turned to the channel receives the signal and with a similar black box converts the noise signal back to a message on a computer screen."

"In other words if you have the right collection of black boxes all you have to do is type in the message on one computer and someone on another computer can read it," King reiterated with a sense of

The Mammoth Incident

understanding and disbelief apparent in his voice.

"Yes, that is the idea," responded Geoff.

"Could these messages be in some form of code?" asked Camden.

"I don't understand, of course the message is encoded by the computer to be an electronic signal," noted Geoff.

"No, I understand that, but I mean is it possible to send a coded message such that anyone else receiving it could not understand it? In other words the transmission be garbled or be secret unless you had the right key to it." Camden tried to explain his concern.

"Yes, I see what you mean. Sure, the message could be coded. Anything you would want to type could be coded and then the cryptic message sent over the airways," responded Geoffrey nodding his head in understanding. "I just would wonder why anyone would go to that much trouble though!"

"Why do you say that?" asked King.

"Well very few people would have this sort of equipment. In fact I can not think of anyone with such equipment. The idea of transmitting information by radio signal never gained wide acceptance in the computer community since the phone lines were handy and it was much easier to use them. They are faster, tend to be more error free and readily available at little cost. The "black box " or phone modem necessary for use is much easier to come by than the equipment we have been talking about," Geoffrey explained with a knowingness that Camden and King accepted. "Is there some relationship between your questions on computers and what is happening in the cave?"

Camden explained his thoughts on a possible connection for the benefit of Superintendent Hicks, taking Geoff's inquiry as the basis to try out his latest speculation on the relationship between the mansion house, the school bus, and the cave.

"It sounds plausible enough given the things Geoff's said about computers and the other incidents you describe... I guess the big question now is what to do about it. Do you want to present this to the security forces?" asked Hicks.

"No way. I don't think they would believe me. Remember we are working with a lot of sheer speculation. There is very little hard evidence to support the scenario I've described... Furthermore if they did believe me they would probably screw the whole thing up, given their track record to this point," an emphatic Camden noted.

King concurred with a nod and a smile and Hicks was obviously swayed by the soundness of Camden's logic. He, too, had little confidence in the security people to this point.

"We have to take out that school bus without them triggering the explosives they apparently have wired into the cave. If we rush them we have to be sure we get them all, otherwise they may blow everything," Camden noted.

The Mammoth Incident

"How do you propose we do that? asked King. "Go up and knock on the door and ask to see their camping permit, then jump them!"

"That is a possibility. Keep talking," suggested Camden.

"Keep talking! That's all I've got," King said quietly.

"Why not tell them to leave?" suggested Geoffrey.

"Sure, tell them they have been evicted and can not stay in the park anymore, " chimed in Superintendent Hicks a little sarcastically.

"No, that is not what I meant. Send them a message in which you indicate the ransom has been paid and that they should proceed to leave the area," Geoffrey suggested.

Struck by the seeming simplicity of the plan Camden at first didn't know what to say and just nodded his head in silent approval. After another moment or two he turned to Geoff and asked, "Think you can operate that equipment at the mansion house or have you got some other source in mind?"

"I believe I can figure out how to operate the equipment at the mansion house with a little luck. I don't have any other source where we could get the equipment needed on such short notice," responded Geoffrey Hicks.

Chapter Sixteen

It was late afternoon when Camden accompanied by Hicks and his son approached the mansion house. The estate seemed very quiet for a summer afternoon. Camden thought it was much too quiet. The main entrance gate was open when they arrived and they had simply driven in. Camden parked the car alongside the garage he had so swiftly exited the day before.

Camden continued to ponder the ruse of "using the phone." The simplicity of the idea seemed inconsistent with the complexity of the situation. Surely walking up to the front door and ringing the doorbell and then asking to use the phone was not going to be a satisfactory basis for accessing the house. However limited, it did seem better than the rather direct, but crude, idea of breaking and entering. The trio approached the front steps apprehensively and eased up to the front door. Camden pressed the door bell button and waited nervously. His acutely aware senses could hear the chiming of the door bell inside. It sounded like Tchaikovsky 1812 Overture, particularly the part with the cannons. To any person in not quite such a hyper state the tones were much more subdued and far from the intensity of the overture, much less the cannons.

Camden waited what seemed like an inordinate amount of time. Rolling over in his mind the opening words for whomever opened the door. "Good afternoon, may we use your telephone?" "Hello, I'm Mick Camden with the Park Service. We

The Mammoth Incident

were in the area when our car developed mechanical problems. May we use your phone to get assistance?" "Hi. I Mick. Stopped by the other night and wanted to apologize about smashing your car." Somehow none of the various opening lines seemed satisfactory. A minute passed, then two, then three... Camden looked nervously at Hicks and Geoff and then back toward the door. His gun hand unconsciously moving toward the holstered weapon, then as he became conscious of his actions he eased his hand back to his side. Another minute or two passed and still no response. Camden reached down and tried the door knob. He twisted and pushed and, to his surprise, the door moved inward with little resistance.

Camden stepped into the foyer. His ears strained to pick up any extraneous sound. None was forthcoming. Conscious of his gun hand under his jacket he unholstered the weapon, released the safety, and held the weapon in a position ready to fire.

The house was exceedingly quiet. Only the ticking of a large grandfather clock could be heard in the entryway. Camden eased forward and peered cautiously around each entrance off the hallway and found nothing. His sixth sense indicated the house was empty and his other five were confirming that through observation and more empirical information.

"It looks as if no one is at home," Camden said.

"Where do you think everybody is?" asked Hicks nervously.

"I wish I knew," said Camden. "But why knock a good thing? Let's get to the radio room and see what we can do."

Camden lead the trio down the hall and up the stairs to the second floor and the studio. As he went he checked each room they passed. Still there was no sign of a soul. The studio was equally empty and the trio eased in quietly.

"Hicks, take a position by that window and let me know if the owners return. I will cover this door... Geoff there is the computer I told you about. What do you think? Can you do it?" Camden asked in a concerned tone.

"It is an Apple IIe as I thought, and the rest is pretty much what I had in mind. Now if I can just find the power switch," said Geoff as he reached behind the computer terminal and flipped a switch. The twin disk drives chirped as the power surged to them. A red indicator light suggested that the right switch had been found. With a little more poking around Geoff had succeeded in activating the printer and the CB radio as well. "So far so good."

Camden sighed to himself. This could turn out to be a piece of cake the way things were going, he thought. His sixth sense, however, was sending strong signals to the contrary that even Camden knew better than to ignore.

Geoff was busily typing into the computer the message Camden had suggested. "I am going to test the transmission on a different channel than the one

The Mammoth Incident

they have been using to be sure I got it working the way we want," said Geoff, as he flipped the knob on the radio to a different frequency. His hand returning to the keyboard he tapped the "enter" button and instantly a brief shrill tone pierced through the room, followed by the clatter of the printer as it typed the transmitted message.

"Sorry about that... didn't realize I had the volume turned up quite so far," Geoff smiled sheepishly as a concerned Hicks and Camden looked on in some anguish. "It does seem to be working and I am ready to send when ever you are, Mick."

"What is going on here?" demanded the female voice emanating from the slender dark haired beauty standing in the doorway holding a chromed .38 revolver. The line of sight ended somewhere in the proximity of Camden's navel, give or take an inch or two. This relationship was not lost on Camden and might account for his lack of a more intelligent response.

"We... er... wanted to use the phone," Camden said as softly and unaggressively as he could muster.

Hicks nodded in support and Geoff didn't move a muscle. His eyes were frozen on the revolver. In his minds' eye the revolver was suspended in space and not connected to anything else. An instrument of death that suggested his own mortality in a very real and profound way that he had never glimpsed, much less even considered, in his young life.

"Easy does it. No sudden moves or you're

dead," the voice cool and controlled suggested to those present that this individual meant what she said. "Move over here," she waved the gun in Hicks direction and motioned him toward Camden. "You... get up from there," she directed to the youth.

Geoff still transfixed by the cold reality of the gun did not move. "What is the matter with you? Move it!"

The bite of her voice cut through the trance and Geoff staggered to his feet. "Yes, sir... What ever you say. Please... Please... don't shoot me," Geoff gasped in a quivering voice that revealed the depth of his fear. The revelation was not lost on the gun bearer or anyone else in the room.

"What are you doing in here? I want answers, not conversation!" she commanded.

Camden was puzzled. He thought he was confronted by Sarah, the Major's daughter who he had been hot tubing with just a few days before. Was she so astonished by their presence that she didn't recognize him? There had not been so much as a hint of recognition and her voice was so controlled that she was not that stressed. But then again being held at gun point demanded mental energies be directed to the immediate problem at hand and not at recognition difficulties of selected individuals.

Almost, subliminally Camden caught a glimpse of a golden flash of light as something shifted under the blouse while her gun hand swept about directing Hicks to the position he now occupied immediately

The Mammoth Incident

next to him. He could not be sure but suspected she wore a Krugerrand on the thin gold chain that lay lightly on her neck.

There was obvious tension in the air as Camden looked at the woman, and the woman looked at Camden. There was a noticeable lurch in the woman's hand when the phone rang. This was amplified by the sensation that swept Camden's body from the surprise to the phone ring so much so that he thought he had been hit fatally by the yet unfelt and unheard bullet from the 38. Fortunately, the sense of imminent doom swept away as fast as it came as his body correctly interpreted the external stimulation to his senses.

She answered the phone on the third ring. Tension in the room was slowly edging down from a new high moments before. After telling the party to hold on she motioned the trio into the walk-in safe in the studio and closed the door. The sound of the tumblers falling was not lost on the occupants in the darkened stillness of their confinement.

Camden pressed against the door to listen, hoping to catch part of the conversation with the unknown caller. His ears were well tuned to the most subtle sound, and the sound of his own breathing masked whatever bits of the conversation that might have made it through the steel door. He did hear a muted click that he took to be the hand piece being returned to the cradle. In another moment the muted closing of a door was also heard. He assumed that the gun bearer had business elsewhere and had departed. Trusting his intuition and the muted sounds picked up by his senses, he turned his attention back to the confines of the safe.

"Have you got a lighter or matches?" Camden asked of Hicks.

"No, I don't smoke... Maybe I should take it up," offered a concerned but still humorous Hicks.

"Well, then we are even," said Camden.

"Hugh? What do you mean by that?" asked Hicks.

"I was supposed to be watching the door... She should never have been able to walk in on us like that. By the way, wasn't that Sarah? She didn't seem to recognize me or you either for that matter," asked Camden.

"It certainly looked like Sarah. But it could have been the Major's other daughter, Serena. While they aren't twins they look very similar and are easy to confuse unless seen together," said Hicks.

Camden pondered Hicks' remarks as his hand moved around the wall surface adjacent to the door. "Ah, here it is!" With that the lights in the room came on.

"How did you know that was there?" asked Geoff.

"I didn't. I just figured they are like everybody else and have to see what they are doing when they are in here. And now for my next trick... I hope my assumptions are just as valid this time," said Camden

The Mammoth Incident

as he started poking and pulling on bits and pieces of the mechanism that composed the safe door locking mechanism.

Hicks and son just stared at the door and Camden in disbelief. Wondering if the strain of the last few minutes was too much and he had gone off the deep end. Their answer came in less than another minute as they heard a latch release and the door yield to Camden's weight pressing against it.

"How did you do that?" asked an astounded Geoff.

"Magic," replied Camden.

Hicks chuckled, "The safe was made to keep people out. Not to keep someone in if the door should accidently close... You are one sharp fellow, Camden. I wouldn't have thought of that in a thousand years."

"Me neither," volunteered Geoff.

His gun drawn, Camden checked the room quickly and then glanced down the hallway to be sure the gun bearer was indeed gone. He thought he heard the muted sounds of a car moving away outside. By the time he got to the window with a view of the drive who ever it was had already departed. Camden returned to Hicks and Geoff still standing in the studio, not quite sure what to do next.

"Send the message as planned. I am going to help King," Camden instructed as he turned to head out the door of the studio. "I'll send a car back for you. I don't think they will be coming back since they know we are onto them. In any event, they will assume we are still in the safe."

Camden bounded down the hall and the stairway to ground level. Just as he was halfway to the front door it opened and in stepped Sarah. Camden froze for an instant as her eyes met his and then instinctively threw himself to the floor with his gun aimed at a point directly between her eyes. His reflex to fire was more than he could check. As the gun went off it was that sixth sense of his that pulled the point of aim the six inches off center sparing Sarah's existence in her current form. The bullet passed diagonally through the partially opened door spewing fragments of wood and glass as it went.

"Mick," screamed Sarah in that shrill hysterical sound that only a woman scared to death can emit. "Why are you trying to kill me?"

Camden was now consciously aware that Sarah, while similar in appearance was not the woman he had encountered earlier. Was not holding a gun and appeared to possess no life threatening capabilities. He pulled himself off the floor and regained his feet.

"I thought you were someone else. Come on, I will explain as we go," yelled Camden. Not waiting for a response he grabbed her arm as he moved by her and pulled her with him.

Too terrified to resist Sarah stumbled along trying to regain her composure as she went. One minute sobbing and submissive, the next biting her lip

The Mammoth Incident

and balking in an effort to resist Camden's pull.

Camden gently pushed Sarah into the front seat of the Park Service sedan saying, "Please... Please trust me... I can explain everything... but not right this moment." Camden wondered if he was sufficiently convincing to Sarah, since he was not convinced himself that he could indeed explain everything.

In any event she seemed to stabilize and rode in mute silence as Camden maneuvered the automobile like a grand prix racer down the drive and back toward the park.

Chapter Seventeen

Camden found King crouched in the tree line surrounding the campground and about fifty yards from the school bus.

"Well, what has happened? Anyone left yet?"

"Nothing, not a thing has happened. Did you send the message?" asked King.

"Yes, about twenty minutes ago we finally got it out. Our earlier efforts were interrupted," answered Camden. "I am going in there."

"Don't be foolish! We don't have any idea how many are in there. And don't know how they are wired in... they may just have to hit a button and all those people in the cave are wasted," explained a concerned King.

"You're right... I didn't mean I was going to take it. More like a little reconnaissance. Cover me..." said Camden as he slipped toward the corner of the school bus moving from one location to another with some sort of obstacle between him and the school bus at all times.

Camden closed easily to within about fifty feet of the targeted corner of the bus. The last segment however was a different story. The area was devoid of any substantial bushes or shrubs and gave no cover at all. Camden surveyed the rear and side window of the bus one more time. From what he could see, they appeared to be painted or paneled over and had not been used as windows for quite some time. A condition he had seen in other old school buses converted to campers. Hoping this was like the others

The Mammoth Incident

in his experience and not the exception to his generalization Camden moved the last fifty feet rapidly but cautiously. Reaching the rear of the school bus he eased himself under the bumper and crawled slowly to a position just behind the rear wheels.

Under the bus bits and pieces of conversation wafted down. Then he heard the fall of feet as someone moved toward the front of the bus. Camden took a deep breath and checked the safety on his weapon. The door of the bus was forward and he heard it open. Apparently he had been seen approaching and an unanticipated and unwanted encounter was to occur.

From his vantage point King could see that Camden had arrived. "All right, he has done it, that old rascal," King sighed under his breath. "Ah shit, now we are in for it!" exclaimed King as he saw the school bus door open. His hand checked the safety on his weapon in anticipation of firing.

An individual emerged from the school bus and walked slowly and directly toward the car parked near by. On reaching the car the individual reached in a pocket and with the set of keys found within opened the trunk of the car and removed a small valise which he carried inside.

King breathed a sigh of relief. Camden also breathed a sigh of relief although his was considerably more muffled than King's.

Camden lay flat against the ground under the bus. He felt he was actually becoming part of the

George R. Harker

ground given the intensity of his mental efforts at concealment. A twitching sensation emanated from somewhere near his stomach. The first signal was barely perceptible, the second not a whole lot stronger but definitely there. "A hell of a time for a heart attack or indigestion," he thought before he realized that the sensation was caused by an external stimuli and was not something internal. This realization stimulated the copious flow of perspiration and a cold chill over his entire body.

Shifting his weight to his elbows Camden eased his stomach off the ground as far as he could given the school bus above. Twisting and contorting his body he caught the glimpse of something curvilinear about the diameter of his little finger moving away. The vivid colors of red, yellow, and black were particularly striking and registered in Camden's mind for further consideration later on.

Camden eased himself back to the ground hoping all other snakes and similar creatures below had ample opportunity to take up residence elsewhere.

"Check the cave again," came a muffled but discernible voice from somewhere above in the school bus.

"Looks quiet, Nothing unusual happening that I can make out," came a muffled response.

"Any sign of conformation on that last transmission from the boss?" asked the initial voice.

"No. I don't understand... It is not like the

The Mammoth Incident

boss not to follow procedures. What should we do?" asked the second individual.

"We won't do anything. You know the Major, he is a stickler for doing things by the book. His book! If that was just a test and we blew it we would have the devil to pay. No, we wait. Two transmissions within five minutes or forget it," the first individual responded. The self assured tone of this voice suggested to Camden that this was the person in charge at this end of the operation.

Camden eased himself out from under the school bus and retraced his steps back to King.

"What's happening?" asked King.

"Plenty! We are on the right track, just have to attend to some details. I'll be right back. I've got to make a phone call. I hope they accept the charges... Don't go away... I will be right back," Camden told a perplexed King before running off in the direction of the administrative complex.

****

Fifteen minutes later, King whirled to the right, his gun hand slicing through the air in a controlled arc of an expert. The full force of his hand could smash concrete blocks or do equal damage to a man's rib cage. The deflected force sent the hand upward and back to the starting position where it was ready to strike again.

"Easy, it's only me," said Camden rubbing the

side of his arm which he had use to deflect King's blow. "I didn't know how to get your attention without startling you. You always get that engrossed in school buses?"

King smiled, "I wasn't expecting a hand on my shoulder under the circumstances."

"Anything happen?" asked Camden.

"No, not a thing. Why? What should be happening?" asked King.

"Hopefully they will be leaving shortly. I just called Hicks at the mansion to send the message in two consecutive transmissions. If I am lucky, that is the key and we may see something happen," explained Camden as he moved alongside King and the two gazed with anticipation at the school bus.

A few minutes passed when the door of the school bus opened and out stepped the individual who had earlier gotten the package from the trunk. He walked over to the car in a rather nonchalant manner, got in and started the engine. He lit up a cigarette and appeared to be waiting for someone. Camden glanced over at King and their mutual smiles conveyed that idea that all systems were go and the "plan" was working nicely. A moment later the school bus door opened again and another male stuck his head out and shouted something to the driver. Camden could not pick up the exact words but sensed it was something to the effect, "Go on without me, I've got a few things to clear up and I will be along shortly."

The Mammoth Incident

"Ah shit," said Camden. "I should have known this was going too easy. One of us will have to go in there and take that turkey. Since I seem to be the one getting paid for it, guess I had better do it."

"What about that guy in the car?" King said. "Are you going to let him get away?"

"He is probably small potatoes and we can catch up with him later. Unless you have a better idea?" Camden suggested.

"As a matter of fact I do have a better idea. To get out of the park he has to circle around behind us. How about if I go out and flag him down and ask him to stick around for a few minutes that we would like to talk with him," King remarked in the sardonic drawl that Camden had come to enjoy in the last few days. Camden wondered just what King had up his sleeve this time and knew better than to ask.

"Sure, go ahead. See if he won't stick around and perhaps join us for coffee," Camden answered.

King headed over to the roadway with Camden lagging slightly to suggest that this was King's show and that he would follow his lead. At the edge of the tree line adjacent to the roadway King indicated that Camden should stay put.

King started to saunter up the roadway just as the late model Ford came into view. Camden eased behind a clump of evergreens curious as to what King was going to do. "Surely, he isn't going to flag the guy down," thought Camden. Whereupon that is exactly what King proceeded to do. He motioned to the driver to stop by holding his hand upward in the universal sign to stop. Amazingly the driver did so and King walked over to the open window on the driver's side.

"Say, could you tell me how to get to the main administration building from here?" asked King.

"Sure," said the driver. "You just head over that way about five hundred feet. You can't miss it." In support of the verbal directions the driver also pointed in the direction of the administration building.

King grabbed the outstretched arm and pulled with all his might. The driver responded by withdrawing and flexing the arm in one smooth motion that brought King crashing into the side of the car door. Next the driver, having secured the release of his arm, thrust open the car door catching a crumpling King a glancing blow to the side about chest high. In another instant the driver had pinned the still stunned King to the payment. Obviously, in full control of the situation the driver shifted his position slightly in apparent preparation to pummel King's head into the ground.

"Enough, turkey," shouted Camden into the driver's left ear. The driver moved only his head and that he turned very slowly in the direction of Camden's voice. On doing so he found he was looking up the barrel of Camden's pistol, not more than two feet from his head. Recognizing that further aggressive behavior would not be tolerated the driver relaxed his hold on King and moved in accord with

The Mammoth Incident

Camden's directions.

A groggy King rolled over and sat up clutching his chest with one hand and feeling for the source of blood on his face with the other. "This isn't exactly what I had in mind," said King meekly in a very soft, almost inaudible voice.

"Are you all right?" asked Camden.

"No," said King, "but I think I will live with some effort on my part."

"Good, you have given me an idea on how to deal with that other turkey in the school bus. Let's get this one a cup of coffee," said Camden.

With the driver securely bound and gagged tucked behind some foliage on the side of the road Camden took the wheel. King crunched down in the back seat as Camden turned the automobile about and headed back toward the campground.

"Are you sure this is going to work?" asked King.

"Are you kidding? I am not sure anything is going to work. We are in this too far to back out. If we blow it we might as well go out in style. We should have the element of surprise on our side. Whoever is in that trailer will associate that other guy with this car and certainly not us," Camden answered reasonably sure that what he was saying had some merit.

"I hope your idea works better than mine. God, am I sore. That guy was going to kill me just for asking directions. What is the world coming too?"

"Get down and be quiet. I will be right out. There is only one left in there and once we take him out we should be on the downhill side," Camden asserted as he rolled the car into the parking space it had just left minutes before. Waiting a few moments to give the occupant of the school bus time to conjure up reasons why the driver would be returning so soon, Camden was careful to keep the door post in such a position that his facial features were somewhat obscure to anyone looking out from the front windows of the bus.

After another moment of waiting Camden decided the moment of truth had come and eased out of the car and up to the door of the school bus, trying to stay as close to the bus as possible so that an occupant casually interested in his presence would not be able to get a discernible look. That, anyway, was the plan; the validity of the rationale would be apparent in a moment.

Camden knocked lightly and tried the door. It was locked. He heard the sound of someone getting up and moving toward the door. Camden pressed himself against the side of the bus away from the door.

"What's going on?" came the voice from inside.

"I forgot something, let me in," Camden sort of covered his mouth with his hand. Trying to be just loud enough to be heard but not so loud that voice inflections would tip the difference to the person inside. The door latch clicked and the door started to

The Mammoth Incident

open. Camden threw his shoulder against the door carrying it open and out of the grasp of the door opener. At the same time he leveled his pistol on a point between the eyes. "Easy does it," he said in a low calm voice.

The respondent to this greeting initially lurched back from surprise and then gaining composure eased his hands upward and stepped back slowly. Camden was pleased by the response. It was exactly what he expected if the element of surprise was on his side and apparently it was. The plan had worked, flawlessly.

On the other side of the bus was a console not unlike the one at the mansion house. A monitor, computer, and other assorted paraphernalia were attached to shelves which lined the entire wall on the driver side of the vehicle. Camden motioned the slim thirtieth year old male to sit down in the chair in front of the computer. Judging from its position in the room it was probably where this person had gotten up from to answer the door. He could not have seen Camden approach sitting down.

"Tell me the status of the people in the cave! Are they in any...," Camden's inquiry was cut in mid sentence by a voice slightly behind and to the left of where he now stood looking at the display on the computer console.

"Ease that gun down fellow or I'll blow you apart," the voice of another male cut through the air like a hot knife through butter.

Camden yielded to his intuitive reflexes throwing himself forward and downward while intuitively aiming and firing at a point about two feet below the sound of the man's voice. The two explosions were so close together that they almost sounded like one. The bullet from the unknown intruder passed through a fold in Camden's shirt and took out the front windshield of the bus. Camden's bullet found its intended mark and slammed the assailant against the side of the bus. Slumping to the floor from the force of the impact the assailant's gun discharged again from the involuntary reflexive contraction of the arm which the bullet had grazed on its trajectory to the abdomen. This second bullet ricocheted off the ceiling and hit the computer monitor with sufficient residual force to implode it. The man seated at the computer terminal leaped on the prostrate Camden pinning him to the floor.

With the wind forcefully expelled from his lungs by the impact, Camden's grip on the gun and life itself weakened significantly. The attacker wrestled the gun from Camden's hand and raised it over his own head in the beginning of an arc that would smash the base of Camden's skull when completed.

The downward swing lost its' momentum and missed the projected point of impact due to an involuntary shift of the attacker's center of gravity. King's foot had caught the man square in the rib cage with the full force of a firehouse kick. The attacker grimaced with the pain of fractured ribs and struggled

The Mammoth Incident

desperately to regain an orientation and some sense of where to point the gun. This attempt at centering was quickly stifled by King grabbing the dot matrix printer and bringing it down with force on the head of the assailant. The man groaned and slumped over into an unconscious heap next to Camden with the printer laying in fractured disarray between.

Camden took a couple of deep breaths to assure himself that he was indeed still breathing and turned to King, "Thanks for not waiting in the car."

"Just returning the favor," King smiled.

"You sure did the job on this one. He is out cold. How about the one I shot? asked Camden.

King had moved over to the form slumped in the doorway. A thin muscular individual with a light build. "He won't be causing any further difficulties. I think he bled to death."

"Let's get this guy tied up and see if we can bring him around. I've got a few questions I would like answered. I wonder if Geoff can make heads or tails out of all this equipment around here," Camden gestured at the array of "black boxes" and monitors that covered the one side of the school bus.

A light rap at the bus door sent a cold chill up Camden's back as he recovered his gun from the floor. "Who is it?" Camden yelled.

"It's Hicks," came the reply.

Camden opened the door and motioned Hicks in.

"Boy, this place is a mess. What have you been

doing to our resident campers?" Hicks jested.

"How did you know to just walk up here?" asked King. "Weren't you worried about getting wasted by these turkeys?"

"I didn't just walk up. It was more like crept up and then I heard your voices through the shot out window and knew you had everything under control," explained Hicks. "Sarah is worried about you. She told me where and what you were up too. I figured I would give you a hand, but you seem to have everything under control. By the way those high muckity mucks in Washington have authorized the payment of the ransom. They were rather demoralized by the mauling the special force took when it tried to take the cave from the inside."

"What's that? You have got to be kidding! Mean they are going to give in and wire the money to that Panamanian bank?" Asked Camden in disbelief mixed with a little anger and contempt.

"No, they are not going to wire it. It seems shortly after the aborted attempt to take the cave another ransom note appeared. This one gave the time and place for a local drop and reduced the amount of cash to just over a million," replied Hicks. "Apparently, they couldn't resist the bargain basement terms and have agreed to the extortion. A FBI agent is off to make the drop. He left just about the time I did to come over here."

"Well, what a turn of events. We are just about in control of the situation and they are giving in.

The Mammoth Incident

Guess there isn't much we can do about it. There are going to be a lot of awfully red faces when they figure out the timing of the payoff and what we have got here. Or at least what I think we have got here," said Camden.

"Mean I took all this abuse," King motioned to some of his more obvious bruises and some miscellaneous cuts and scratches, "and they are still going to pay those bastards off? I wonder if we can work out a deal? Maybe the thugs will split the money with us if we let them go."

"Now there is a thought worth considering," said Camden with a smile.

"There is one thing funny about this latest ransom note that has been really bothering me," said Hicks.

"Well, don't keep us in suspense what is it?" asked Camden.

"The drop site for the money is in Wild Turkey Hollow," replied Hicks.

"So, what is the big deal about Wild Turkey Hollow? You've seen one hollow you have seen them all. Haven't you!" offered Camden.

"For the most part that is true. But I happen to be pretty familiar with Wild Turkey Hollow, and this one is a bit different. The Park Service was checking it out for a possible group camp site a few years ago and I spent some time there. We finally decided not to use it because there was only one way in and out. To get access to anywhere else in the park you had to walk about three miles back down the single road in to get out. Most any other hollow in the place you can, with a little effort, climb up the adjacent hills and head off into some other section of the park. Not so with this hollow. The surrounding limestone bluffs are not climbable except with equipment," said Hicks.

"I see, so it would be a good place to see who is coming but you think the person or persons picking up the money would have trouble getting out, unless they climb up the bluffs," Camden speculated out loud. "These people seem to have a knack with technology so climbing the bluff would probably not pose any big problem... Where did you say this Wild Turkey Hollow was located?"

"I didn't," said Hicks as he glanced around the room for something he had seen earlier. "This map should show it." Hicks removed a map stuck near the smashed computer console and placed it on a small table between them. "Yea, here it is. It is not named on this map but this is the hollow. You can see how the road snakes in here." The closeness of the contour lines at the upper end clearly showed the hollow to be as steep as Hicks had indicated.

"Well, I wondered what our guys will do? Do you think they plan to send in a crew up the front or perhaps have a team circle in behind on the ridge top?" Camden speculated out loud.

"Neither," said Hicks. "The intent is to do absolutely nothing. Remember, the brass still thinks

The Mammoth Incident

the terrorists have the upper hand and with the decision to pay have decided not to attempt a capture as long as people are pinned in the cave. Given their perception of the situation, this is probably not an unreasonable position to take."

"Well, let's get back to getting the hostages out of the cave. How is our hostage doing?" Camden turned to the man on the floor who was just beginning to stir ever so slightly. "Don't try anything, the odds are clearly not in your favor."

"What hit me?" came a somewhat meek inquiry for a hurting person.

"Just a Japanese import," Camden said with a smile and pointed to the smashed Epson printer on the floor. "Have you been monitoring and controlling all activity in the cave from this console?"

"I've got nothing to say without my lawyer," replied the injured man.

"Perhaps you would like to reconsider that last question," said King as he reached down and picked up the main portion of the printer and lifted it above the head of the recalcitrant.

"All right, all right I'll tell you what you want to know. Just don't hit me again," a more talkative recalcitrant answered.

"Do you monitor and control all activity in the cave from this position or are there other locations as well?" Camden asked again.

"Everything in the cave is handled right here," answered the man.

"Are you sure?" asked King flexing the arm holding the printer.

"Yes, I swear it," came the reply.

"Would you get your son over here to see if he can make this place operational? Tell him to be careful and not do anything until I get back. Above all tell those shitheads from Washington to sit tight until I get back. Tell them under no circumstances are they to send anyone into the cave until I return," said Camden directing his remarks primarily to Hicks.

"I understand, but where are you going?" asked Hicks.

"I just got a hair-brained idea I want to try... are you coming King?" asked Camden as he picked up the map showing the location of Wild Turkey Hollow.

"What... does a bear shit in the woods!" King answered. "Where is it we are going, partner?"

"How about a little chopper ride?" answered Camden.

Chapter Eighteen

"Sorry, sir, we are under orders to stay on the ground until further notice. I think it has something to do with the ransom payoff. You understand that last part is unofficial and you didn't hear it from me!" the helicopter pilot explained.

"I see. Well, I am afraid I must override those orders," responded Camden.

As the captain listened in astonishment to Camden, King walked quietly around the chopper disconnecting tie downs and removing all other impediments to flight. Then he quietly slid into the pilot's seat and hit the starter button. The rotors began to move.

"What are you doing?" screamed a perplexed captain.

"Sorry, we are just borrowing your bird for a few minutes. You did all you could to stop us. Don't try anything more or it could get serious," Camden said in a very commanding tone as he brandished his gun long enough to be sure the captain had been properly coerced into relinquishing the control of the copter.

"As you like, sir. I yield to your superior fire power. Clearly a higher authority," smiled the Captain. "Good luck! Sir."

Camden returned the smile and ran around the front of the chopper and climbed in next to King. "Are you sure you know how to fly this thing?" asked Camden.

"If it's got wings, I can fly it," responded King.

The rotors began to whine as they picked up momentum. The craft shuddered, then lurched into the air.

"This thing doesn't have any wings!" exclaimed Camden as the craft barely cleared the edge of the administration building at the edge of the parking lot.

"Is that right... then we are in trouble," King smiled and acted like he had given up flying right then and there, throwing his arms up in total despair. Just as the chopper appeared to be going out of control he came back on the stick and the chopper resumed a straight and level attitude that Camden equated with normal controlled flight. Camden breathed normally again.

"Remind me to never question your flying abilities again," Camden said in a voice King could hear above the engine noise as the machine lumbered skyward.

"South southeast was the direction, wasn't it?" questioned King.

"That is an affirmative. It should be just a couple of hollows ahead if my dead reckoning is correct," responded Camden glancing from the map to the terrain below and back trying to pinpoint their location. "There, eleven o'clock. Doesn't that look like it to you?"

"Got it! That's a roger. That is a `turkey' hollow if I ever saw one. Check out that cloud of dust," King motioned to a point off to the right.

"We must be too late. That must be the drop

The Mammoth Incident

car and it is going the wrong way. They must have made the drop already. Can we raise them on the radio?" asked Camden.

King flipped a couple of switches on the instrument panel and a digital readout showed an array of numbers in fluorescent orange. "This knob here changes the frequency. Here is the mike. Try 136."

"Chopper to mobile unit in Wild Turkey Hollow. Chopper to mobile unit in Wild Turkey Hollow. Do you copy?" Camden paused and waited a few seconds before repeating the call.

"This is mobile unit in Wild Turkey Hollow, go ahead," came a voice over the helicopter radio.

"What is status of drop?" Camden asked.

"Affirmative, drop has been completed as per instruction," the mobile unit answered. "What happened, I thought we were to maintain radio silence?"

"Change in plans regarding radio silence. Say again drop location," shot back Camden as if the first part of the transmission was not relative.

"Dropped per instruction, middle of the turnaround at head of Turkey Hollow," answered the voice on the radio. "Say, I thought you knew that? Why are you asking?"

"Just routine follow-up. No problem. Chopper clear," Camden said in his most matter of fact tone. Turning to King "Can you take this chopper over the center of the canyon? I want to see if the money is still where they left it. It is supposed to be in the middle of that turning circle down there."

King maneuvered the craft over the canyon and held it stationary as Camden scanned the turning circle looking for anything that resembled the suitcases which would contain the ransom money. "Can you take us lower? I don't see anything suggesting the ransom money," Camden shouted above the roar of the engine.

King acknowledged with a smile and brought the machine low and to one side of the clearing. He purposely was keeping the craft over the forest to minimize the impact of the down draft. At first Camden did not understand what he was doing but then caught on as the copter circled the clearing giving a clear view from all angles. There could be not doubt. The money bags used in the drop were not there.

"Take it up and keep your eyes peeled on the ridges. The money is gone and who ever got it must be trying to climb out. If they have a vehicle down there it is well camouflaged. With just the one way out that doesn't seem to make any sense, anyway," Camden yelled over the drone of the engine.

King nodded affirmatively and as the chopper raised it also spun about on its vertical axis giving Camden a clear view of the rock facings on the adjacent cliffs. There was no sign of the anticipated climber.

"Perhaps they are holed up," said King. "After

The Mammoth Incident

all, we are not exactly invisible up here."

"Take it up a thousand feet. You gave me an idea with that `holed up' comment. After all, this is cave country, maybe they went underground," said Camden.

Responding as requested King couldn't help but wonder, "How is going up going to help us locate them if they went underground?" So he asked.

"I'm not sure I know. Just make ever increasing circles and look for somebody or something out of the ordinary," said Camden.

The first loop took them around the perimeter of the hollow and supported the premise, at least in the sense that no one was climbing out. If they had been it would have been most apparent given the lack of cover on the rock faces surrounding Wild Turkey Hollow.

Flying ever increasing circles, King was just about to start the third circumference when Camden spotted something. In the next hollow to the west of Wild Turkey he thought he saw the glint of light from a car windshield. King abruptly circled the chopper for a closer look nearly throwing Camden out the door in the process. A secure seat belt prevented disaster.

"Good thing you had that seat belt on," said King.

"Why didn't you tell me you were mad at me?" answered a cajoling Camden. "What do you make of that van down there?"

"Nothing, just some campers in the hollow.

We've seen it time and again these last few days."

"Yes, that's true. But something is different. There doesn't seem to be anybody around. I don't see a tent or other signs of a camp. Nothing. In the past the tent or campfire was right there in close proximity to the van. One thing for sure around here is that people don't like to get too far from their vehicles," said Camden.

King nodded in agreement, "You got something there, partner."

"I can't be certain but there is something about that van that is awfully familiar to me. Perhaps it is just the paint color, but I could swear I've seen it before," said Camden.

"What do you want to do now?" asked King. "You think this is what we are looking for or should we keep on looking?"

"You're right! I am not certain and there doesn't seem to be any activity. Perhaps this isn't what we are looking for. Lets keep circling, but keep this van in view as best we can," said Camden.

The ever widening circles took the copter over the next hollow. Camden's eyes strained to catch any deviation from the normal that might indicate the presence of the extortionist. "There under that tree!" exclaimed Camden.

King responded as if by reflex tilting the copter in an angle that gave Camden the most unobstructed view possible from that particular place in the sky. Then slowly he even changed the sky

The Mammoth Incident

location to enhance the view. Moving the copter quickly into the best view angle possible given terrain and other obstructions.

The enhanced view yielded a clearer look at a station wagon. The rear gate was extended. Nearby, the canopy of an umbrella tent filled part of the clearing. Two children paused from their play to get a better look at the strange and noisy craft hovering overhead. Breaking off the approach King turned the helicopter back to the original flight line without Camden needing to say anything. The van in the next hollow clearly didn't fit the mold.

"It's gone!" a surprised Camden shouted above the engine noise. The intensity of his response startled even King who was ready for most anything, but not this. "Look, it's gone."

King focused his eyes in the direction of the clump of trees where the van had been parked. Nothing. He changed the direction of flight bringing the chopper over the hollow in less time that it takes to tell about. A cloud of dust lifted softly from the road bed in the hollow and was beginning to settle back down. The down draft of the chopper sent the dust billowing even higher than it had before.

Down the hollow the dust cloud converged. At the moving apex of that convergence the cream colored van Camden had seen under the trees moved at a moderately brisk pace.

"I've got a feeling that who ever is in that van is the person we are looking for. Can you keep them in sight without them knowing we are up here?" asked Camden.

"No problem. If we stay high and generally behind it will be quite difficult, if not impossible, for them to see or hear us," said King.

The van slowed at the junction at the mouth of the hollow and then rolled the stop sign. A common practice in the area and not necessarily indicative of a person in a hurry. Even on the hard surface road a few miles further on the car did not speed excessively but kept close to the posted limit. The driver was confident and apparently not taking any chances that would bring an unwanted encounter with a traffic cop.

"Army ground control calling Army helicopter two niner four. Come in," the radio crackled to life.

"Might as well answer them. See if they have an additional information," said King.

"OK. What frequency should I use?" asked Camden.

"Try the one you were using to contact the car. I expect they are monitoring it and a few others," replied King in a matter of fact manner.

"This is army helicopter two niner four. Come in, ground control," said Camden into the mike.

"King is that you flying that chopper? You are in illegal possession of government equipment, and I order you to land that thing back here immediately," came the voice of someone rather indignant with King.

The Mammoth Incident

"Ground control, have you got any additional information on the ransom payoff?" Camden responded, ignoring the previous transmission.

"You are not listening two niner four. Bring that helicopter back immediately or I will have you court martialed," the voice was louder and more belligerent than before.

King took the mike from Camden and said, "Your last transmission was breaking up. Please say again in slower more audible tones." As the obviously exasperate ground control operator began to repeat himself in louder and more exaggerated manner, King flipped a couple of switches and the radio receiver went dead. He looked at Camden and smiled. Camden returned with a smile and directed his attention back to the cream colored van below.

"Isn't that the road to the airport?" asked Camden as the cream colored van turned off the highway nearly out of eye range.

"Yes, I do believe you are right. Shall we meet them on the ground? They will take a while to wind up the canyon. We can be on the ground at the field in less than five minutes," said King.

With Camden's implied concurrence the helicopter increased forward speed and started to descend rapidly. Within minutes King had neatly dropped the chopper behind a hangar opposite the main entrance to the field. The cream colored van was nowhere in sight. And the hangar would obscure detection of the chopper from all but the most astute observer, assuming, of course, that they entered through the main entrance.

"What do you want to bet that DC-3 is involved in this?" King asked.

"How about a million in small bills in a couple of suitcases?" said Camden.

King secured the main rotor which had finally stopped rotating of its own accord. Then he joined Camden who was watching for the cream colored van around the edge of the hanger.

"What is the plan?" asked King. "You going to open up on them as they pull in? Or are you going to jump out in front of their van and tell them they are under arrest?"

"Your point is well taken. Actually I had hoped to catch them in the act of moving the money. Then with their hands full, to move on them. Got any better ideas?" asked Camden.

"Not necessarily, but here is one you might want to consider. It is actually a variation of what you have suggested." King went on to explain his idea of being on the plane and taking out the terrorists when they least expected it.

The water closet on the DC-3 was refurbished as was the rest of the plane's interior. Never-the-less it was still intended for use by a single occupant at any one time. The tight quarters brought Camden and King into a more intimate contact than either desired.

"We are going to look pretty silly if this isn't their plane and part of their plan," said King.

The Mammoth Incident

"It could be worse, we could still be up in that stolen helicopter," Camden said.

"You got something there. I think I hear something..." whispered King. The rear door of the aircraft opened and the folding steps could be heard clanking into position. It sounded like one person was on board and that suitcases or some other luggage were being passed up by a second person outside the plane.

A moment later the folding stairs could be heard retracting into the plane. Then the door was closed with a solid thud. The latching mechanism could be heard as the securing bolts found there respective slots.

It seemed to Camden that the two had moved forward to the cockpit in preparation for take-off. With pistol drawn Camden eased the latching handle counter clockwise and pushed the door to open. Instead of easing open, the door remained securely in position not budging an inch. Thinking he had not applied enough force. Camden eased his full weight against the door through the application of his left shoulder. Still nothing, the door would not budge. Camden looked to King who was as puzzled as he.

"What did you do? Lock the door?" asked Camden.

"Yea, I didn't want to be walked in on," said a sarcastic King. "It must be jammed. That happens occasionally on some of these internal doors. Perhaps the partition containing the door got out of alignment."

The left engine of the vintage DC-3 coughed to life. In another minute the right engine joined the first and the plane began to roll out of the hanger.

"It was a great plan if only we could have taken them out while on the ground. Now we will be here until they land or have to take a leak which ever comes first," said Camden.

They could feel the aircraft roll out onto the concrete. The increased whine of the engines indicted to King that the preflight ground checklist was just about complete. The engines backed down for a moment as the plane turned on to the threshold of the runway. The whine of the engines increased perceptibly and the aircraft began to roll.

"I do believe we are taking off," said Camden. "This is one fine kettle of fish you got us in, Olly."

The plane climbed perceptibly and banked steeply to the right as the pilot took a non-standard departure from the airport. The bags stowed in the rear of the plane in front of the washroom door shifted slightly. Camden thought he heard the noise of luggage shifting and tried the door again. This time it opened easily and moved about six inches before meeting resistance of the baggage. Camden leaned on the door with his full weight again, and the bags slipped enough to permit exit. The step climbing turn had toppled the bag which had so effectively wedged the door shut.

Camden barely squeezed through the door and

The Mammoth Incident

was about to head forward when he noticed the doorknob to the cockpit compartment start to turn. Not wanting the confrontation to occur prematurely and on less than his own terms he pulled back into the washroom and eased the door shut. Fortunately, King was as agile as he was tall and moved quickly against the washroom wall when Camden unexpectedly reversed directions. Camden held his gun ready in the event the washroom was the destination of the person coming his way.

In what seemed to be a rather long time, but was only a minute or two Camden could hear the movement of baggage right outside the door. He braced himself for the encounter he momentarily expected. Nothing happened. In any event the door was never opened or even tried. He waited wondering what was going on. Perhaps the person was just reorganizing the baggage. In any event a potty stop was not the concern.

A few more minutes passed with Camden pressed against the door trying to figure what was happening outside. All he could hear was the moving of luggage and an occasional fragment of speech. "Here, use this." "Put it here." "That ought to do it." The disjointed phrases made no sense at all. Then he realized that who ever was outside was talking to someone else. The realization that two people were just outside the door provoked the obvious question: "Who was flying the plane?" While Camden had not seen who had gotten on board his senses had never doubted for a moment that only two people were involved, no more or no less. As his mind churned over the events of the last few minutes to validate this premise or allow for something overlooked, his introspection was broken by the sound of the door latches releasing and of air racing across the opening where the door of the DC-3 had been. About the time his conscious mind realized what he was hearing a voice shouted "Now" above the roar of the slip stream. Camden was not sure but he thought he felt a slight tremor in the plane a second later and then within another few seconds another. He listen intently and could hear neither the sound of baggage being slid about or anything else above the sound of the engines and the noise of the slip stream racing by the plane.

He cautiously turned the knob on the washroom door and eased the door outward, ready for an encounter with the unknown persons. The door lurched from his grasp and he turned to face and destroy the person responsible. There was no one there to destroy for the wind coming through the open door had created a powerful eddy which had wrenched the washroom door from him. He turned quickly and moved forward to check the interior of the plane for the people he expected to find. None were present. King stood at the open exterior door and motioned to Camden and then pointed downward. Returning to the door Camden saw two white parachutes deployed below.

"Who is flying the plane?" asked Camden.

The Mammoth Incident

"Automatic pilot."

Camden looked at King with a quizzical look which prompted a smile and a reply from King: "You should know better by now."

"I didn't say a thing."

"You were thinking it."

"No, I was thinking I would feel a lot better if you were at the controls rather than some automatic pilot I don't even know!"

King moved up to the cockpit of the aircraft and took over the controls. "Let's brighten the day for our two sky divers," said King, as he did an abrupt 180 and dove the DC-3 straight toward the two.

One of the parachutists looked visibly moved and began pulling on the parachute cords in an effort to take the chute in a direction at right angles to the aircraft. The second seemed noticeably calmer and Camden began to wonder why. He did not have to wonder long for the thud of metal on metal explained everything. The second chutist had drawn a revolver and was coolly trying to shoot down the DC-3. The third bullet cracked the front windshield of the craft as King rolled the plane slightly to assure that the parachutists were not snagged as the plane thundered between them. He intended only to start the adrenalin flowing and not to kill anyone or himself through an intentional collision. The impact of even one parachutist on the fuselage or wing surface of the DC-3 could be enough to bring them all down. He had not really reckoned on being shot at either and this turn of events negated any thought of another pass. The DC-3 started to circle and climb to a safer vantage point.

"Did you see what I saw or am I seeing things?" asked Camden.

"Yea, I see it. He was shooting at us and he hit us," replied King puzzled by Camden's question of the obvious.

"No, not that. I mean did you recognize the parachutists?" asked Camden.

"I wasn't paying that much attention. But now that you mention it I do believe I have seen them or at least one of them before," responded King. "The one doing the shooting looked a lot like the Major. The other looked like a woman."

"What do you bet? It fits. The brains behind this whole operation was the Major and that is him floating away with his less than lady-like daughter, Serena," Camden concluded.

King was busily adjusting dials on the instrument panel as Camden watched the parachutes float lazily to the ground. Within minutes of landing in a large field below the chutes disappeared from sight. Apparently gathered by the parachutist and not left in haste as a marker for others to follow. Camden tried to find a reference point that would bring him back to the right field. But once the white canopies disappeared he could no longer be sure exactly where they had landed.

Meanwhile King had determined the

The Mammoth Incident

coordinates of their location and headed the aircraft back toward the airfield from which they had come.

The left engine began to sputter and miss emitting clouds of blue black smoke as it did so. King immediately feathered the engine and applied more aileron to offset the drag created by the loss of power from the failed engine. "While I'll be darned, it seems like that turkey got that sucker," said King.

"What are you telling me? You mean that person shooting from a parachute took out our engine with a handgun?" said a disbelieving Camden.

"I can not be certain but it sure looks that way," replied King.

"Now what? Are we going down?" asked a concerned Camden.

"No, not till we are ready. These babies could routinely fly on one engine if they had to. They are one hell of a good plane," remarked a confident King. "We should be over the field in another ten minutes in spite of our difficulty."

Camden sat back in the co-pilot's seat and tried to relax. While he had come to acknowledge King as an expert with regard to anything that had wings, he still felt uncomfortable looking at the wind milling left engine.

A few minutes later Camden's train of thought, actually more of a meditative trance, was broken by the sound of misfiring in the right engine. "Good Lord! What is happening now?" asked Camden in a voice which didn't hide the terror in his heart.

"It appears that we are about to run out of fuel," answered King in a very matter of fact and nonchalant manner that suggested he did not perceive this as any great difficulty. "This is Douglas niner niner five calling Mammoth field."

"This is Mammoth field. Go ahead niner niner five."

"Both engines out. Attempting dead stick landing runway one nine. Entering downwind shortly. Niner niner five."

"No reported traffic. Runway one nine clear at the moment. Do you want a fire truck?"

"Negative on fire truck. No fire. Would like to be picked-up if possible. Emergency situation. Need your assistance. Niner niner five."

"Roger, will pick up. Good luck. Mammoth field standing by."

King trimmed the aircraft and turned crosswind to line up for his final approach. Banking through the final turn, the threshold of the runway appeared and looked very comforting to an apprehensive Camden. So much so that he sighed an audible cry of relief which even King could hear. King smiled and made minor modifications on the trim of the aircraft. Just above the threshold of the field King pulled back on the controls to achieve the flare needed to set the ancient aircraft gently on the ground.

King's technique was flawless. However, on touching the runway the left tire chose to blow out.

The Mammoth Incident

Forcing the landing gear into the asphalt at an angle and force far greater than it could handle. King tried to shift the weight of the craft to the other gear with the use of the ailerons. But there was little he could do since the slowing of the plane diminished the effect of the control surfaces to a point they had become ineffective.

As the gear collapsed under the weight, the plane spun around in a shower of sparks. Pulling to the left the dragging wing-tip tore out a series of runway lights and chunks of turf. In less than thirty seconds the forward momentum of the craft had fully dissipated, and the dented fuselage sat at an unnatural angle off to the side of runway one nine. A pickup truck raced down the runway to assist.

The rear door of the aircraft opened and King stepped down onto the grass. Immediately behind him followed Camden. His calm collected external appearance belied how he felt inside.

"Are you all right?" asked the truck driver and airport manager.

"No problems. Would you fuel this baby up? We want to leave for Houston as soon as we go to the bathroom," King casually answered with a smile. The truck driver just shook his head as they got in and headed for the cluster of buildings that was Mammoth field.

Chapter Nineteen

As Camden drove up to park headquarters he could see groups of men with picks and shovels all ready to dig out the captives. All they appeared to be lacking was the final order to do so. Camden felt relief that the powers that be had waited as per instructions and not done anything further. While he could not articulate why, Camden had this uneasy feeling that any premature attempts to re-enter the cave would result in the needless deaths of more innocent human beings.

The campground had been cordoned off and a roadblock and sentry placed at the entrance. Camden had just mentioned his name and was immediately signaled through with the clear acknowledgement that he was expected.

Inside the school bus Geoffrey sat in front of the computer screen as the screen flashed different images, some text and some illustrations. A number of people gathered around looking over his shoulder. Camden moved up through the group so that he could also see the screen. "What have you got?" he asked.

"Oh, hello Mick. Glad you are back," responded Geoffrey. "Just looking over some of the materials we found here and also some we brought over from the mansion house. It seems the people responsible for this were very meticulous and had thoroughly researched out many aspects of the cave. What they had found out they saved on these disks." Geoff motioned to a couple of boxes of disks sitting on the shelf next to the computer terminal.

The Mammoth Incident

"What are we looking at right now? It looks like a schematic of the cave," said Camden.

"Yes, that is what it appears to be. Look at the detail. It even shows the location of the remote cameras and the electrical cable that interconnects them," acknowledged Geoffrey with a smile of satisfaction on his knowledge of the symbols used in the working drawings appearing before them.

"Yes, I see. That dashed line is clearly tied in with the video cameras. What is this one here that seems to run along the side of the cave but is not tied into anything?" asked Camden.

"Gee, I don't know. It appears only in this one portion of the cave. The portion where everyone is trapped. Look, it begins or ends behind this boulder in this portion of the cave and then runs down to the far end where it either begins or ends behind another large boulder," said Geoff.

"What do you make of those 'x's' marked on that line? They appear to be more closely associated with that end of the line farthest from this point over here," Camden pointed to the end of the line which was also in close proximity to the area where he had previously entered the cave.

"I don't have any idea. Whatever it is appears to begin and end right in this section of the cave. In all the other diagrams the lines representing wires ended in one section of the drawing were picked up in the next section," said Geoffrey.

"Let me see some of the other diagrams," said

Camden. Geoffrey hit some keys on the keyboard and different sections of the cave appeared as three-dimensional line drawings in some cases with others being two dimensional longitudinal cross sections. "You say there is nothing like this particular diagram in any of the others?"

"I can't be certain. But in the few I have looked at there are none with lines that don't appear to connect with the next in the series," Geoffrey said.

"I've been looking over Geoff's shoulder through most of this and I believe he is right. Basically it looks to me like we are looking at a wiring diagram of the cave, with each line running back to some location outside the cave... either park services headquarters, our power source, or the wires put in by these people which all come back to this school bus," superintendent Hicks' spoke softly, but with a sense of conviction that Camden had learned to respect. The man had seen lots of wiring diagrams of caves, particularly this one and knew what they meant.

Camden was sure there was something significant about the mysterious unconnected wire. Just what it was, however, eluded him. "I've got to go back into the cave and find out what that wire is about," said Camden. "Besides there is somebody in that cave who is not a captive but rather a plant. That person has to be identified and taken out before any more damage is done."

"What should we do with these digging crews?" asked a man who before had been giving orders in

The Mammoth Incident

superintendent Hicks' office with little regard for Hicks or Camden.

"Good question! Give me an hour's head start, then send them in through the main entrance," replied Camden. "Are you coming with me?" Camden turned to King who was standing against the wall just inside the door of the bus. King was so quiet that few people realized he was there until Camden called their attention to him.

"I best not, partner. I tend to be a bit claustrophobic," King said with a joking manner that Camden had come to know was quite serious. Camden nodded understanding and left with superintendent Hicks to pick up some cave equipment.

"You must be King," said a man in an army uniform. "I'd like to ask you what you did with our helicopter."

King smiled, "Have you got a box to put the pieces in?"

Chapter Twenty

Camden felt like he knew the path back into the cave by heart and that he could travel it blindfolded if needed. While much of the trail was becoming second nature to him, he was surprised at the changes that had taken place at the breakdown. Large pieces of rock which he remembered as being farther up the slope now were lodged at the bottom. Depressions and piles of rock and dirt around some of them gave mute evidence of valiant efforts by some to extricate others caught in the rock slide triggered by the terrorists. Clearly, the swat team had no expectations of what was coming. Nothing in their training could have prepared them for this possibility. Camden moved up the slope thinking about the men who had died here, recalling his own close call just days before. What hand of fate let him live while others died? Camden moved through the opening at the top of the breakdown and eased down the chimney to the ledge accessing the main portion of the cave.

From his vantage point Camden could see much of what was going on in the cave. For the most part things seemed about the same as he had remembered them. He dropped off the ledge and looked behind the rock corresponding to the one in the wiring diagram he had asked Geoff about. Running just under the sandy surface Camden found a wire just like the one he had found earlier in the main cave entrance. Remembering that situation, he surmised exactly what the wire was for and cut out a

The Mammoth Incident

three foot section which he rolled up and placed into his back pocket. He then walked nonchalantly into the group much as if he was returning from satisfying a call of nature. No one seemed to be particularly aware of his presence. The days of confinement had brought with them a sense of resignation and boredom. People played cards and tended to other mundane matters in an effort to help the time pass. The movement of people to and from the makeshift rest rooms was a continuing phenomena of little interest to most.

As Camden approached Milly he motioned with a subtle movement of a downward palm to be calm. Which she did with great difficulty, since her inner feelings were one of joy and relief on just seeing him. He explained to her that rescue was imminent but that an effort must be made to find the terrorist planted in the group. After briefing Milly, Camden picked out a comfortable rock from which to observe the group and particularly the large boulder near where he had entered. Within fifteen minutes he and everyone else could hear the sounds of digging outside the blocked passageway.

Milly announced what everybody had already realized. It would be just a short matter of time and their captivity would be over. The mood in the cave was quite different than when Camden entered. It had become more animated and more lively. People seemed to be joking although others seemed to be holding back tears of joy and relief. Others were openly crying, unable to hold back their emotions any longer.

Camden nearly missed it since his attention had been momentarily diverted by the particularly emotional outcry of one young woman. But out of the corner of his eye he had seen someone slip behind the boulder he had been so intently and discreetly watching.

Quickly and quietly he walked over and rounded the boulder with gun drawn and ready to fire. A man of about thirty and trim build was on his knee's behind the boulder connecting a small black box to the ends of the wire protruding from the sand floor of the cave.

"Set the box down," directed Camden.

The man winced slightly from the surprise of being confronted by Camden, but quickly regained his composure and turned and looked up to face him. "No, you put the gun down or all those people will die," said the man with the detonating box connected and the trigger button under his thumb.

"Don't be foolish. There is no reason those people have to die. Just put the box down and give it up," said Camden.

Without further hesitation the man pressed the button. When nothing happened he rapidly rechecked the connections seemingly oblivious to Camden or anything else. He pressed the button again and then again. Still nothing happened. It was becoming apparent to Camden that this individual was becoming livid with rage and was about to single handedly pull

The Mammoth Incident

the whole cave down if that was going to be what it took.

Camden reached in his pocket and produced the three feet of cable he had earlier snipped from the line. He threw the cable in front of the crouched figure. "Why you son of a bitch", shouted the man at the same time throwing a handful of dirt in Camden's eyes. Camden's gun instantly discharged more from reflex than conscious thought. The bullet missed by inches and smashed into the cave wall.

The pent up frustration and rage in the man was finding an outlet in savage punching and kicking of which Camden was taking the brunt. The gun had been smashed loose on the initial impact and now lay in the sand a few feet from the scuffling duo.

As skilled as Camden was in self defense he was unable to counter all of the attack. The speed and savagery of the aggressor was taking its toll on him. His body was starting to give out, and he found himself flat on his back and pinned by the assailant who was now trying to choke him with some success.

One second Camden thought he was going to lose consciousness and the next he thought the aggressor had slumped over and off of him. Camden lay still unable to move or comprehend what was happening. Was he indeed unconscious and this is what it felt like to die? His blurred vision was starting to clear and he saw Milly standing over him and the attacker. In her hand was a rock about the size of a cantaloupe. She dropped the rock and bent over

Camden.

"Are you all right?" she asked.

"I am not really sure.. Did you do that?" Camden asked gesturing weakly toward the prone figure next to him.

"Yes, he was trying to kill you and it looked like he was going to succeed unless I did something," said Milly. She helped Camden to his feet and gave him a gentle bear hug.

Camden found the hug invigorating and realized he had developed a greater attraction toward Milly than he had previously realized. He also found he had a lot of aches and pains, some new in the last few minutes and some from earlier in the day. The cumulative effect was such that he wondered if he could still walk. With Milly's assistance he walked slowly back to the rock he had been sitting against earlier and sat down. In the background he could hear the sound of the rescue team as they dug. It may have been his imagination, but it seemed the sounds were getting closer. Perhaps it was not his imagination and it would be just a matter of time. Camden slipped into the unconsciousness of sleep.

Chapter Twenty-One

"Where am I? What is going on?" Camden asked as he awakened to the sound of medical corps men muscling the wheeled litter into the back of an ambulance. Through his half opened eyes he could see Milly's soft face with the long brown hair streaming down. The lighting was soft as the last rays of an afternoon sun filtered through the pines surrounding the parking lot closest to the main entrance.

"You are going to be all right," said Milly in a soft reassuring voice. "They just want to take you to a hospital to give you a complete check-up and be sure you are OK." Milly held Camden's hand as the corps men locked the litter into position for transport.

"I am fine, just a bit tired... That's all," Camden lied, becoming aware of a few muscle aches and pains he was trying to ignore. "I'm not going to any hospital." So saying he loosened the strap across his waist, intended to keep him on the litter, and sat up. His head was spinning a little bit so he held himself steady waiting for it to clear or at least subside. In a minute or two it did. The dizziness was more the result of getting up to quickly rather than any physical problem. Milly attempted to encourage him to go to the hospital, but when she saw he was clearly not going to have any part of it she helped him step from the ambulance.

"I didn't think they could cart you off that easily," said a smiling King standing just outside the ambulance. "Steady, partner." King eased up alongside Camden and took some of the weight that was resting on Milly.

"What happened?" asked Camden.

"Well, they got everybody out of the cave. Thanks to you, that terrorist in residence wasn't able to set off the charges and cut out through the side entrance like he planned. Only three of the hostages died. One was a terrorist and he doesn't count. The others were a pharmacist from a small town in Illinois and a farmer from Iowa who just happened to be in the wrong place at the wrong time," explained King.

"What about those two who jumped from the DC-3?" asked Camden. "Was that the Major and his daughter Serena like we thought?"

"Seems to have been," said King. "Looks like the Major was into the international scene, in ways none of us can fully appreciate."

"Are they going to catch them?" asked Camden.

"Don't know if they are going to get them or not. The police got to a ground site that matched the coordinates I gave them and found the chutes stuck under some shrubs. However, the two seem to have got away. They don't have what they think they have. The dollar amount in the satchels was considerably less than the million they were expecting and all the bill's serial numbers are known. If they start spending it the Feds will know it," King explained further.

"Sounds like things are under control. I could sure use a hot shower and a little R&R," Camden said softly turning to find Milly's brown eyes answering the

The Mammoth Incident

implicit question in the way he had hoped. "See you in the morning, King. Probably about time we fly back to Washington."

"I left a little surprise for you in your room. It is a tape the terrorist made that you and Milly might enjoy," said a smiling King. "See you in the morning."

Camden looked at Milly in puzzlement and Milly returned the look equally puzzled.

In the room Camden found a wheeled cart containing a color TV and video recorder with a tape already in place. The machine was already plugged in and positioned for easy viewing from the sofa or the bed in the small efficiency apartment that was Camden's abode since arriving at Mammoth Cave.

After a shower Camden curled up with Milly to spend a relaxing evening together. "That King has my curiosity aroused. What do you suppose is on that tape that would make him think we ought to see it tonight and not some other time?" said Camden.

"It does seem a little strange. There is one easy way to find out," said Milly as she gingerly hopped out of bed and hit the "on" button of the TV and started the tape rolling.

Camden had propped himself up with a pillow and was enjoying the visual aspect of the smooth contours of her body as she returned to join him. He realized he had never seen her nude except in the rather subdued carbide light in the cave. Initially the screen of the TV was filled with spatters of color and the sound of static. Then the picture cleared and in darken hues the forms of two people making love could be seen. The imagery was not the best, but it was clear there was a lot of intensity in the relationship being witnessed. Camden looked at Milly and Milly returned the look as both realized that the lovers on the screen were in fact themselves. There in the depths of Mammoth cave big brother had been watching their every move including their most intimate relations. Their initial shock gave way to amusement.

"Why watch when we can have the real thing?" said Milly as she hopped out of bed to turn off the machines with Camden's full approval.

Milly hit the off button on the recorder and the TV screen filled with the local program. Just as she reached for the button to silence it:

"WE INTERRUPT THIS PROGRAM TO BRING YOU AN IMPORTANT NEWS BULLETIN - TERRORISTS HAVE STOLEN 3 POUNDS OF HIGH GRADE PLUTONIUM FROM THE NUCLEAR FACILITY AT FORT KNOX. WE REPEAT..."

Milly glanced at Camden for reaction. Seeing none she switched off the TV and returned to the bed.

Camden took her into his arms and began to savor the warmth and smell of her body. His mind oblivious to everything but the woman he was with. He began to whisper words of love but to his surprise he heard his own voice saying: "I'll be damned! This

The Mammoth Incident

whole thing at the cave was nothing more than a diversion. The real target of the terrorists all along was the plutonium."

Milly knew he was right but she also shared a sense that some things could wait until morning, and the two went back to making love as if nothing had happened.

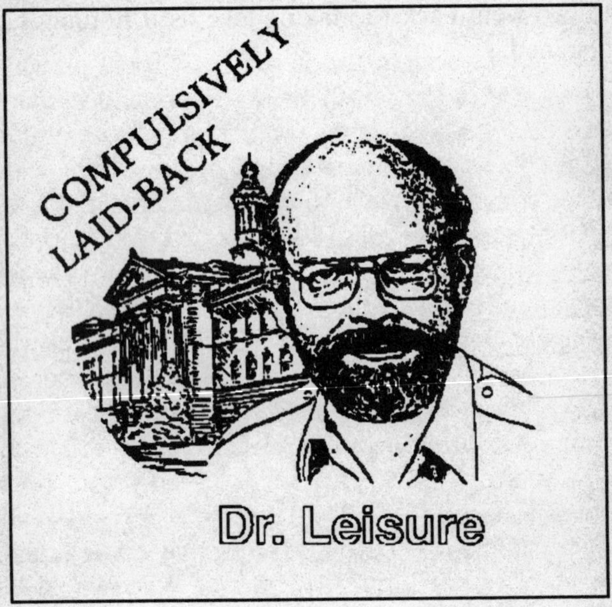
COMPULSIVELY
LAID-BACK
Dr. Leisure

Author's Note

This book was written in 1984. It grew out of a workshop sponsored by the Faculty Development Office of Western Illinois University. The workshop was entitled "Integrating Personal and Professional Goals" or "IPPG."

It was designed to help faculty focus on what they wanted to get out of their careers and perhaps more importantly what they wanted to get out of life. I had achieved some success at the university receiving more grants and teaching more students than my departmental colleagues. Yet I wanted to do more. I was looking for something that would open up other opportunities. During the workshop I realized that my one main ambition with the greatest potential was "write a book." I had started the project years before but never got very far. I made completing the book my number one priority. In the six months following the workshop I did indeed complete the book presented here.

Little did I know in 1984 that my considerable success in research and teaching at WIU would be viewed with such envy and jealously that a very concerted effort would be made to drive me from the department and the university. The conspirators successfully achieved their objective. I was the first tenured professor to be fired from WIU on June 20, 1991.

I wrote a book about that conspiracy entitled, *He Wouldn't Drink the Hemlock: The Firing of Dr.*

Leisure. With the publication of that book I also became a publisher. I have also published the work of Abdi Sheik Abdi, another former professor at WIU.

Coming across the manuscript for *The Mammoth Incident* while searching for some other documents I thought, why not publish this story? So I did! I hope you find it interesting and fun to read. It was fun to research and write. Remember proceeds from the sale of this book will be used in an effort to re-establish the concept of academic freedom within institutions of higher learning in Illinois.

George R. Harker
Macomb, Illinois 61455-1247

A Word about Dr. Leisure and his press:

Who or what is Dr. Leisure? Dr. Leisure is the registered trademark of Dr. George R. Harker. Dr. Harker is a philosopher and teacher. For twenty-one years Dr. Harker taught such courses as the Philosophy of Leisure while affiliated with Western Illinois University.

Successfully fired by jealous colleagues in 1991 it became apparent that the philosophical teachings of Dr. Leisure was the basis for his dismissal. Dr. Leisure's focus on the teaching of Aristotle was apparently not "politically correct" at WIU in 1991.

But given the profound effect that Aristotle's teachings have had on the very foundations of this country it is not surprising that the teachings and message of Dr. Leisure is very relevant to contemporary society. After all the pursuit of happiness is part of the cornerstone underpinning what this country is supposed to be all about. Or at least it was in the beginning of this great nation. Today more and more individuals are trying to come to grips with the meaning and significance of their existence. The teachings of Aristotle and Dr. Leisure are helpful in that endeavor.

As a publisher Dr. Leisure is committed to the betterment of the human condition. Works from Dr. Leisure Press may range from very sophisticated intellectual treatises to just a plain good adventure read. It seems that all are important to the human condition.

Have an idea for a book and don't know what

to do with it. Or better still have a manuscript ready to go with no publisher. Contact Dr. Leisure to see if a joint venture might be the way to go.

Dr. Leisure International

Books by Dr. Abdi Sheik Abdi

Dr. Leisure is proud to be the publisher of Abdi Sheik Abdi. Dr. Sheik Abdi was born in Somalia. Educated in the USA and a US citizen, he has written a number of books about his homeland.

Tales of Punt is a collection of eight Somali folk tales as retold by the author.

When a Hyena Laughs is a novel about a youth growing up in Somalia that wants to escape his rural existence and go to the city.

____ Tales of Punt $11.95
     ISBN 0-9638802-2-5 (paper)

____ When a Hyena Laughs $14.95
     ISBN 0-9638802-6-8 (paper)

____ When a Hyena Laughs $29.95
     ISBN 0-9638802-5-X (hard)

order from:

Dr. Leisure
13 Cedar Drive
Macomb, Illinois 61455

Please state your name and address and include $3.00 for shipping, handling and tax per order.

The Adventures of Dr. Leisure

Coming soon to a book store near you are the adventures of Dr. Leisure. Adventures will include stories that are fiction and some that are fact. All are based on the real life adventures of Dr. Leisure. Dr. Leisure has travelled around the world on two occasions and visited over twenty foreign countries. He has been in all fifty states. His mode of travel has included auto, train, plane, boat and hot air balloon. As one person who knows Dr. Leisure put it, "Dr. Leisure lives other peoples' fantasies."

Share the adventures of Dr. Leisure. Look for the first of the series at your local book store in the next few months.

Dr. Leisure's True Life Adventure Stories

The cornerstone book of the true life adventure stories series is *He Wouldn't Drink the Hemlock: The Firing of Dr. Leisure*.

First published in 1993 it is the true story surrounding the firing of a tenured professor from Western Illinois University. The professor, Dr. George R. Harker, had established himself as an expert in nude recreation by researching the state regulations regarding nudity in all fifty states.

The request for Dr. Harker's expertise took him to exotic parts of the world which included Hawaii, Thailand, China, France and some twenty other foreign countries. Colleagues upset with jealousy and envy took it upon themselves to force him from the university. Eleven obviously trivial charges were brought against Harker. Even though it was known the charges were not valid he was still fired.

If this story were fiction it would be viewed as implausible. However, it is fact and it may be a cliche but truth is stranger than fiction.

Order from: Dr. Leisure, 13 Cedar Dr. Macomb, Illinois 61455, *He Wouldn't Drink the Hemlock: The Firing of Dr. Leisure*. ISBN 0-9638802-1-7, 461 pages. $12.95 plus $3.00 shipping and handling.

Dr. Leisure Memorabilia

Since the inception of Dr. Leisure in 1992 a small but growing cult of supporters has sprung up. In response to that interest various items have been produced which carry the Dr. Leisure logo and message. Such items include shirts, sweat shirts and mugs. Interested in a more complete list of items and prices? Send a self addressed #10 envelop to Dr. Leisure, Macomb, Illinois 61455-1247.

Dr. Leisure Shirts

Very unique! Printed on both the outside and the inside. Yes, it is reversible!

One side features compulsively laid-back Dr. Leisure with university administration building on the front. On the back, "Don't have a seizure, listen to Dr. Leisure."

On the other side is compulsively laid-back Dr. Leisure and nude maidens of Little Beach, Maui. On the back the slogan is, "It's a pleasure with Dr. Leisure."

Black print on grey cotton/polyester tee shirt. Available in large and extra large. Cost is $15 per shirt plus $3.00 shipping and handling per order.

Mail to Dr. Leisure, 13 Cedar Drive, Macomb, Illinois 61455-1247.

COMPULSIVELY LAID-BACK

Dr. Leisure